HITTER AND BLUE

HITTER AND BLUE

D.C. Schulze

Copyright © 2023 D.C. Schulze

All rights reserved. No part of this book may be reproduced in any form or by any electronic or mechanical means, including information storage and retrieval systems, without permission in writing from the publisher, except by reviewers, who may quote brief passages in a review.

Paperback: 979-8-9872754-0-5
Ebook: 979-8-9872754-1-2

First edition

LCCN: 2023901950

Hitter and Blue is a work of fiction. The names, characters, businesses, places, events, locales, and incidents are either products of my imagination or used in a fictitious manner. Any resemblance to actual persons, living or dead, or actual events are coincidental.

To Cindy, Katie, and Kyle, my home team.
And to the dogs.

"SPIKE"

The abandoned property at 730 Paxton Avenue has been many types of houses over the past nine years. It has been, in no particular order: a party house, a flop house, a drug house, a house of ill repute, a gambling house, and, most recently, a dogfighting house. What the property has not been for a long time is a home.

After Miss Ida Pangley passed away in her sleep one unusually cold night in May 1970, her prized pink one-story structure had been boarded up tight. Now, dark and crumbling, Miss Ida's place looks much like a dozen other houses on the same city block.

Every padlocked door, each shuttered window, serves as a reminder of the hard times that have befallen the good people of Paxton Ave.

Long ago, the city had placed a large red sticker on Miss Ida's front door reading: "PROPERTY

UNINHABITABLE—KEEP OUT!" At the moment, however, there is one lone inhabitant. Spike, a three-year-old pit bull terrier, moves wearily through the house's gloomy hallways.

Starved by his owner to a "fighting weight" of forty-five pounds, the dog is jet-black—almost blue—with patches of white on his front paws and chest. His head and shoulders carry the half-healed scars of a dozen deadly fights. Shallow breaths show as frosty puffs in the cool night air.

Searching for a way out of the house, Spike claws yet again at the front and rear doors, without success. In the kitchen, he licks a few drops of condensation from a rusted water pipe beneath the sink. At the basement stairs, he stops to peer into the blackness below. Shivering with cold and fear, the fighting-dog considers his choices.

Perhaps there's a leftover scrap of food down those stairs, or a half-filled water bowl, or maybe an unlatched window, and beyond that freedom and a warm place to spend the night, and . . . No.

Nothing, no power on earth can force him back into that basement. Memories of fights and beatings and angry men with sharp needles and sharper voices swirl in the dog's exhausted mind.

Feeling faint and needing rest, Spike turns for the back bedroom and the tattered old mattress that has become his sanctuary. There, he will curl himself into the filthy fabric that provides a bit of warmth and sleep—or dream of sleep—and wait. There, he will freeze to death, or starve to death, or some combination of the two, and not a living soul will know or care what happens there.

There, on an unusually cold May night, on the floor of Miss Ida Pangley's bedroom, at 730 Paxton Avenue, Chicago, Illinois.

"SPENCER"

"Your father used to surprise you by making pancakes on Sunday mornings."

My mother tells us this and waits for our reaction.

I don't remember it. My sister, Kyla, two years younger than me, remembers everything, and doesn't remember it either. The only surprises I remember from my father are bruises, fist-sized holes in the walls of our trailer, and broken furniture. Those happen so often that they're not surprises anymore. A real surprise would be if he suddenly stopped raging on my mother, my sister, and me.

My mother made up that story to make us feel better, I think. Or herself. Or maybe it really happened, who knows? Either way, it's her way of saying, "He wasn't always like this, I swear."

I hope she made it up, though, because I don't want to believe my father might, possibly, have once been a good man. Now that I have a plan, I don't want to change my mind about him.

Especially today.

It's early, just before eight in the morning, and my sister's getting ready for school. I should be sitting in first-period English, but instead I'm at our kitchen table, the one with the wobbly leg that I keep tightening into place. Why am I at home instead of school?

That's a story for another time; I can't talk about it right now.

With no classes to go to, I have to fill up my day—also part of the plan. Staying busy keeps me from thinking too much. If I stop to think, I might change my mind. Whenever I think of changing my mind, I picture my mother and sister huddled together on the couch while my father shouts and breaks up the place. That gets me right back on track.

I've learned a few things from my father through the years. Things like how to hit, and how to take a hit, and even how to feel trouble coming by that electric tingle in the air when something bad is about to happen. I'm feeling that electricity now.

Meaning—tonight my father is going to learn something from me.
    But I can't talk about it right now. It's a surprise.

ONE

Four hours later I've got a cramp in my writing hand but don't stop to stretch it out. For most of the morning, I've: stared at a blank sheet of paper, read my comic books, watched a little TV, and walked laps around our house trailer.

Now I'm working like a madman to finish my essay, which I absolutely have to have to get back into school next Monday.

It's a Friday morning in May. It's also day three of my three-day suspension from Halvdale Junior High, and I've got to be out of here by noon. My mother's cleaning up the kitchen. She's offering "helpful" advice that I don't really hear as I finish groveling on paper.

If I grovel enough, I'll be allowed back in class for the remainder of the school year.

"Just take your time and do it right," she says, followed by, "You know, if you didn't get into so many fights, you wouldn't be suspended in the first place." To make sure I'm listening, she asks, "Are you listening, Spence?"

Either her voice is beginning to get through or my conscience is catching up with me. "I want to finish it so it's not hanging over my head all weekend," I say.

Am I the type of student who finishes assignments ahead of time so they're "not hanging over my head"? In a word, no. I'm the type of student who doesn't finish assignments.

But I'm motivated. After meeting Monday morning with my guidance counselor, Mr. Schmink, and the principal, Ms. Lepton, I'll have fourteen days of classes until graduation. If I make it through with no missed days and no infractions, I won't have to repeat eighth grade.

Fourteen days versus another year. A deal I'll take anytime.

There are strings attached, I know. Summer school, for sure. And there's the essay, telling how I've learned from my mistakes, and how I'll never get in another fight in junior high, cross my heart and hope to die, et cetera, et cetera.

In most places, and most times, staying out of a fight for a couple of weeks sounds pretty easy. But that wouldn't apply to this place and time.

The time is 1979. The place is Bent Oaks Mobile Home Village, just outside Halvdale, Illinois. Halvdale is two hundred miles south and a whole universe away from Chicago.

Around here everyone fights all the time. It's like a hobby for everyone from the parents on down. The fathers and stepfathers hit the kids, the bigger kids hit the smaller ones, and, in households like mine, the men hit the women too.

I'm wasting time daydreaming. It's 11:55 a.m. and I scoop up the essay and bring it to my room. Maybe I can revise it later. Right now I have to get out of here.

Working my way back to the kitchen, I open the fridge. My mother asks if I'm hungry. She tells me to stop by the diner later for a free meal, before the dinner rush. But I'm not looking for food. I'm checking my father's beer supply.

There, on the second shelf, is an ice-cold twelve-pack. Perfect. I may not be the kind of student who worries about his homework, but I am the kind of son who checks his father's beer count.

Today, more than ever.

Usually, I worry when I see too many cans blocking the little light at the back of the shelf. This time I just smile. A dozen should be more than enough.

Pulling on a sweatshirt, I ask my mother what shift she's working. "Three to closing," she says. "I'll be home by nine."

"And Kyla?" I ask, checking on my little sister.

"Going to Loraine's straight after school. She'll be home at nine, too."

"Good," I tell my mother, without saying why, because she already knows why.

Looking out the window of our trailer, I can see my father's station wagon kicking up dust on the road leading to our front door.

"I'll try to stop by for a bite," I say as I turn for the back door. Stopping for a moment, I almost blurt out what I'm thinking. Instead, I open the door and hurry down the four steps to my bike. I can hear the station wagon pulling to a stop in front of our trailer as I pedal away from the back.

"Spence, where are you going?" my mother calls after me.

But I'm already gone.

TWO

Two young men climb the rotting fence and approach the back door of 730 Paxton Avenue. Locked.

Tremaine Collins knows his mother has a vivid imagination. For years, she's pictured the old pink house across the alley as a center for all types of illegal activities. Now she swears she can hear a baby crying in the abandoned property. татар TC, as he's known in the neighborhood, can't convince his mother to ignore a crying baby. He does convince her, however, not to call the police. Those kinds of calls usually just bring trouble to the caller.

TC has more reliable backup in mind, his friend Michael, and they're soon crossing the backyard opposite his and looking for a way into the old pink house.

TC's mother vaguely remembers the old lady who lived at 730 years ago—Ida something or other.

But for most of TC's nineteen years, the house has sat vacant.

Vacant except when it isn't. At those times, the house hosts all manner of criminal activities, and TC's mother forbids her son from going anywhere near the place. Tonight, she gives him permission to investigate the sounds across the alley but to be "extra careful and get back quick."

Finding a loose basement window, Michael "convinces" it open with a couple of well-placed kicks. Soon, TC is sliding into the darkened space below. The gloomy cellar gives him the creeps, and he hurries two steps at a time up the narrow staircase.

In the living room, TC pulls a blanket from an old curtain rod, allowing a bit of light into the room. There are piles of debris everywhere but no unusual smells. No unusual smells is good. He tries all the windows, searching for one that might open.

On the porch, Michael finds the front door closed, but the padlock hanging open in its clasp. He steps inside where TC is hard at work on a window.

"Need any help?" he laughs.

Surprised, TC turns to face the open front door. "Maybe my mother's right. Somebody's got a key to this place."

"Yeah, and maybe they'll be back soon. Let's look around and get out of here," Michael says.

Following the beam of his flashlight, TC studies his surroundings. The kitchen and bathroom are dirty but otherwise empty. The same with the first and second bedrooms off the hallway. An eerie feeling creeps up TC's spine. He suddenly wants his mother to be dead wrong about this house.

More than the basement, more than the many bad things that have happened in these rooms, the thought of finding a baby here chills him to the bone.

He almost turns and runs. But another thought stops him. The thought of having to tell his mother that he hasn't checked the entire house.

At the end of the hall, TC takes a deep breath outside the third bedroom. The feeling is stronger here, and before he enters the room, TC knows there is, or was, a living being here. With the flashlight gripped tightly in his left hand, he steps inside.

The light reflects the twin pinpoints of Spike's eyes, gazing back from the mattress on the floor.

From the dog's point of view, neither of the two figures in the doorway looks like "the bad man," and that is good. Too weak to protest, Spike lets himself be carried from the room by the young men, through the fence, and back across the alley to TC's mother's house.

Going to sleep sometime earlier that night, Spike had thought, hoped, that it might be for the last time. He knew he should hang on. His mother had taught him to never give up and to always hope. But in his three years of life, he's seen too much, felt too much pain, and simply wants to sleep.

Spike has known only one home in his short life, a harsh one. The man who owns that home, "the bad man," is Jeremiah Lime, who owns many dogs like Spike and treats them all cruelly. Sometimes, Lime brings the dogs to different locations, like this house, where they are forced to fight against other dogs. In that house or this one, men—and they are almost always men—laugh, cheer, and jeer while dogs often die. So it is remarkable for this dog, in this house, to simply trust these young men.

But trust he does because that is the nature of dogs.

TC's mother offers the dog a bite of meat loaf, which he refuses, and a few sips of water poured from a glass into her hand, which he sips slowly. Right now, the dog looks weak and scared. He's "the baby" TC's mother heard crying. TC knows that with a few days of food, water, and rest, he'll be up and around. This dog, with those scars and muscles, doesn't look like his mother's idea of a house pet.

TC decides he had better get busy. He figures he has those same few days, maybe a week, to find a new home for the dog he's already named Blue.

THREE

It's a nice day, lucky because I'm going to be out for a while. I ride past Miller's place, forgetting that he's in school along with everyone else. I cruise the back roads of Bent Oaks for a few minutes before heading into town.

Bent Oaks is a big, I mean huge, trailer park on the outskirts of Halvdale. There are 306 trailers, Miller and I counted them once, on forty acres of prairie criss-crossed with rutted gravel roads.

Everyone around here knows about the Oaks: the social workers, the ambulance drivers, the truant officers, and especially the cops. Mostly, you just say you're from Bent Oaks and you don't have to say much more—people have already made up their mind about you.

I don't usually tell people where I live, unless I've known them awhile and I trust them, like my guidance counselor. I guess Mr. Schmink already knew my address from my file, but he never mentioned it until I brought it up one day.

Mr. Schmink lives over in Halvdale with his wife and kids. Most of the kids in school are from Halvdale too, and a small percentage live in Bent Oaks. That's just the way they drew the map when they built the school. I'm pretty sure the Halvdale parents would like to redraw that map someday.

Halvdale's the kind of town where the fathers come home from the office and read their mail and have a coffee or a soda or something, and then at dinnertime they ask the kids how their day went. On weekends, they cut the grass and coach Little League or Pee Wee football, and after the game the whole family goes out for pizza and a movie.

That's in Halvdale.

In Bent Oaks, the men spend the weekends working on cars that won't start, or moving stuff around in some ready-to-fall-down shed, or going over to the junkyard to pick up parts.

Lots of beer is involved.

Cigarettes, too.

Usually, there's a lot of yelling back and forth from the street to the trailer at their wives or girlfriends about something that's really private, so of course, they have to shout about it for all the neighbors to hear.

Sometimes, the yelling turns into something worse, like hitting. When that happens, a neighbor finally calls the cops, and, presto, everyone disappears for a while. A couple of hours and a few beers later, another fight might start up a block away with a different guy and a different wife.

Right now there's a recession going on. "The Recession of '79." They say things get even worse around here when the economy turns bad, although you might not know it because to me it looks like a recession all the time.

I'm not sure what happens out there in the rest of the world, but I know what happens if you stay in Bent Oaks. You end up finishing high school, or not, and get a job working the night shift out at the foundry. That's if the economy ever recovers and they go back to running full shifts. Then, after a few years on nights, they switch you to days, and after a couple more years, you get your own wife and your own trailer and you spend your weekends cleaning the shed, running for parts, and working on your truck.

And if you have kids, you hit them. That goes with the territory.

I swear, though, if I have kids, I'll never hit them, ever. If I even thought I would, I'd go out to my cleaned-up shed and get my rifle and blow my brains out.

That's what Miller's father did. But it wasn't feeling guilty about hitting the kids that caused it, because he hit them all the time and it never seemed to bother him, so I'm not sure why he did it. I'm not sure Miller even knows why. He told me once that he wished his father would die, and then, after he did, he felt bad for wishing it, like it was all his fault or something.

Maybe I should make a wish like that. I'm not superstitious—I don't believe in curses or spells or voodoo, but nothing else seems to be working.

Anyway, I'm in no particular hurry now that I'm away from home—and my father.

My schedule's all messed up because of the suspension. Nobody's around. Nobody my age anyway. The only ones out are some of the usual porch-sitters.

I recognize a toothless guy and his semi-toothless wife sitting in front of their trailer, smoking cigarettes and drinking beer. I haven't seen them since last November. There was a tarp on their porch all winter covering their patio chairs and the little table that holds their beers and ashtray.

Maybe they were under there too, waiting for the spring thaw.

For a second, I worry about running into a truant officer, until I remember that I'm suspended. I don't think there's a law saying I have to spend my suspension at home behind closed doors, which maybe I would, except for my father coming home early.

If my schedule's been off for the last three days, his has been off for the past couple of months. Since the recession, he's been cut back to twenty hours a week at the foundry. He's home a lot more, and it's hard to stay out of his way.

Lucky for me, I've got somewhere to escape to that no one else knows about. My mother doesn't know where I go and my father doesn't care, so, as my little sister would say, "It's just between three people: me, myself, and I." Every day after school and every Saturday for the past six weeks, I've been pedaling two miles out of town—toward Quentin Road.

After leaving the Oaks, I ride the shoulder of the two-lane for a few minutes, through town and back out again, into open country. Passing my uncle

Ray's house, I can see his car parked in the driveway. Ray is my mother's brother and he's both like and unlike my father.

Like my father, Ray's an alcoholic. Unlike my father, who is an angry guy drunk or sober, he's a happy drunk.

Ray works at the foundry, like my father, but not in the same department or the same shift, which works out for both of them since they're not exactly buddies. Ray was already part-time before the recession hit; he drinks so much that he can't work a full-time job.

I don't know how he's paying his bills now.

I also don't know why his car's in the driveway. He lost his license over a year ago and shouldn't be driving, but I guess he does sometimes.

I like Ray, even though everything he says comes out kind of twisty. Things like, "Wherever you go, there you are," or "Doin' nothin' is hard—you never know when you're done."

But the last thing Ray said to me recently was right on: "Watch out for your father now that he's home more often." My uncle told me that if things ever got "really bad" to gather up my mother and Kyla and to get all three of us over to his place quick.

So those are the family choices: a happy drunk or a mean drunk. I remember when I was about nine asking my mother if Ray could move in with us instead of my father. She frowned and said, "Why not set your sights a little higher?" When I asked what that meant, she said, "How about a life with no alcoholics at all?"

But I couldn't think like that back then—or even now.

Around here, there's a tavern on every corner where the men go to drink whiskey and beer and forget about the recession, and the gas lines, and the layoffs. Or maybe they drank even before all those things. I don't know. I know my father always did.

Still does.

FOUR

I cover two miles quick and arrive at Pal's Place Animal Shelter. Rolling my bike up the side drive, I knock first and let myself in the back door. I catch Josie by surprise. Lately, she's used to seeing me every weekday, but never this early. When she asks why, I tell her it's Teacher Institute Day, which she maybe believes or maybe doesn't, but she's always glad for the extra help.

Josie tells me I've lucked out. "Cleaning's all done. Looks like a nice day for dog walking."

Out walking the dogs is when I do my best thinking. Heading out to the kennel, I get started. Usually, I walk the dogs in groups of three or four, but today I've got lots of time and a beautiful day, so I grab two leashes and open the first two cages near the door.

Right now, there are twenty-eight dogs at the shelter. Fourteen walks at thirty minutes each, plus a break for a meal at the diner should get me back home a little after eight o'clock tonight. Perfect.

On Quentin Road, I'm remembering my first day at the shelter about a month and a half ago. Leaving school on a cold day, I was pedaling hard to get my body heat up. After a while, I noticed this place I hadn't seen before. From the road it looked like just another old brick farmhouse.

That's if you didn't see the sign, or notice the kennel out behind the house. In a car, with the windows up, you wouldn't hear the dogs barking either, but you sure could on a bike.

Hearing the dogs got my attention right away. Mostly because I'd been wishing for one for years and asking for one for months. Not from my father. I knew that was hopeless, so it was my mother who I pestered about it every so often and, later, every day. Here was a place right near our house that had a sign that read "Dogs Available for Adoption."

Turning my bike around, I pedaled back and forth in front of the property. Finally, I stopped out front, pretending something was wrong with my chain. I fooled around there for a while until I saw a tall lady walk from the kennel to the back door of the house.

Something pushed me up her front steps. The next thing I knew I was knocking on the door. The tall lady greeted me. I'm one of the tallest kids in my class, but she still had me by a good three inches.

"Need help with your bike?"

I was embarrassed. She'd seen me hanging out on the road. "Oh, no, my bike's all right. I was just wondering what it takes to adopt a dog?"

I smiled, she didn't, and I was wondering why I'd stopped here in the first place.

"The first thing it takes is someone eighteen or older to sign the papers," she told me, still no smile. Just then the phone rang and she pointed me to a chair inside while she crossed to the kitchen to answer the call.

I was glad for the phone call; it gave me a minute to think. I looked around the place and tried not to eavesdrop on her conversation. Something about a lost dog. Both her kitchen and living room had been turned into an office, with a desk in the living room stacked high with papers, and the kitchen table holding the overflow.

I noticed a sign above the back door that read "NO HUMANS ALLOWED." Hanging next to that was a twelve-gauge shotgun in a rack.

A big pit bull terrier came over, sat down, and just stared at me.

Finally, the lady finished her call and walked over. "You're Sandy MacElliott's boy," she said. I swear my mother knows everyone in town.

"Yes, ma'am," I answered.

"Yeah, that won't work," she said.

"Won't work?" I thought. . . . Was she playing with me before letting the big pit bull tear me to pieces? Why hadn't I just kept on pedaling?

"The ma'am thing. My name's Josie Steele. What's yours?"

"Spencer, ma'am, I mean, Josie. It's Spence."

"Well, Spence, Pal seems to like you and that's a good start." And almost like he knew what we were saying, the big pit raised his paw for me to shake, so I did. "Follow me," Josie said, so I did that, too. But I didn't know where, or why.

Josie pulled on a jacket and led me out the rear door. We headed toward the kennel with Pal leading the way. Stopping at the kennel door, Josie looked me in the eye and said, "You're not afraid of dogs, are you, Spence? I've got some tough-looking guys in here, but they're all sweethearts."

"No, ma—Josie, no worries." I gulped.

"All right, cover your ears," she said before leading me inside.

The noise was crazy loud as a couple dozen dogs all ran to their cage doors, barking like mad. The cages had cement floors, but each one had a blanket and a dog bed, and every bed seemed to have a favorite toy or some other trinket. Each cage also had a rear door, dog-sized, to let the pups out to a fenced area behind the building.

Josie ran her hand over the gates, letting the dogs lick her fingers, before opening half the doors. Out came half a dozen pit bulls, a couple of beagles, a Chihuahua, and four or five other breeds I couldn't name. A few seconds later, I was being spun around by a dozen sniffing, jumping, slobbering, tail-wagging balls of energy.

The dogs bounced off me like pinballs.

I could feel Josie watching as I reached out to scratch ears and pat heads of all different shapes and sizes. "They like you too," she shouted. "That's good."

Josie herded the dogs back into their pens one at a time, then did the same with the dogs in the other cages. Opening a side door, she led me outside to walk the rest of the property. Pal stayed with us the whole time.

About halfway across the yard we stopped. Josie looked down at me again, still not smiling. Now I thought, "Jeez, she's four inches taller than me."

"Okay, Spence," she said, all serious. "That was a test. Don't worry, you passed." She followed that up with "Who else in the family wants a dog, besides you?"

I did some fast talking to convince her that my sister, Kyla, wanted a dog, which was technically true, and my mother as well, although she'd already told me no way, unless I stayed out of fights at school and brought my grades up. When it came to my father, I said something like, "He doesn't mind, as long as Kyla and I take care of it."

Technically, very not true.

Long story short, Josie told me that until she met everyone in the family and both adults signed the papers, the answer was no.

But she offered me a chance to volunteer at the shelter as often as I wanted, warning me, "There's more to it than just playing with the dogs. But, if you're interested, come on by. If you work enough hours, later you can choose a dog to bring home. I'll pay for his vet bills and neutering and send you home with food and water bowls and a leash—the whole thing."

I listened, trying to look like I hadn't already made up my mind.

Josie told me exactly what she was looking for as we walked around the garden, past the chicken coop, and in and out of the small barn. "Mainly, I need help with the dogs," she said. "Walking, cleaning cages, picking up poop, all that glamorous stuff."

She was kidding me, I thought, and even now I'm never quite sure when she is or when she isn't. Anyway, it sounded all right to me, working at a place where the animals outnumbered the people about twenty to one.

Josie went on, "But every now and then I can use a hand with the horses and goats and chickens, feeding and cleaning out stalls and such." I was still interested, but a little confused, like how did you clean up after a horse? Josie must be a mind reader because she grabbed a long-handled shovel leaning against the barn wall.

"Just like the dogs, only bigger," she said. "And I save the horse droppings to fertilize the garden. In here." She lifted the lid off a tall plastic drum filled with horse manure and laughed as I jumped back from the smell.

"You'll get used to it," she told me.

I guess I always thought when I got my first job there'd be a lot of forms to fill out and probably a uniform with a stupid hat or something. Now it seemed like all I had to do was show up and work.

Working every day after school and doing homework with the rest of my free time wasn't the world's worst idea. I hadn't had a better one in a while, and I said so.

Josie asked when I could start.

I said any time would be fine with me.

She asked, "How about right now?" and I said, "Sure, okay," and that's how I ended up pedaling home a few hours later, tired and hungry, and feeling good for the first time in a long time. That was six weeks ago and I haven't missed a day since.

FIVE

Clarkson County, Indiana, is blessed with some of the richest soil in the Midwest. Farmers here say you can drop a bag of seeds on the ground in the spring and come back for your crop in the fall.

At first glance, Jeremiah Lime's spread of 140 acres looks much like the farms of his neighbors. Neat and prosperous.

A closer look and two unusual features might catch the eye of anyone passing by on Seven Hills Road. One is the small forest of oak trees surrounding Lime's house and barn. The second is the tall iron gate blocking the drive.

From a bird's-eye view, a different picture of Mr. Lime's property comes into focus. The gate blocks access to the house and barn, keeping out unwanted visitors. The trees hide a series of sheds and outbuildings not visible from the road. That is not an accident.

Built up over twenty years, Lime's dogfighting empire has grown from a single fighting ring to half a dozen structures covering two acres of land. The main crops in the area, for both Mr. Lime and his neighbors, are corn and soybeans. But Lime has a third cash crop, one that he keeps hidden from the outside world—dogs.

Occasionally, before a big fight, Mr. Lime likes to give his out-of-town guests a tour of the compound.

Behind the house, he points out a low-slung building that serves as a kennel to two dozen dogs. Across from that is a large shed, the training center for the dogs. Here, treadmills and a practice ring compete for space with painkillers, steroids, and antiseptics. Looming behind the shed is a rustic barn, heated and air-conditioned for all-season use, with two custom fighting pits, bleachers, and a bar.

The farmers around Clarkson have all heard the rumors of what goes on "out there." How five or six times a year, a parade of cars turns up at Lime's place, and how the cars are allowed through the gate blocking the drive. Very few locals have ever gotten past that gate. Occasionally, a neighbor who has some business with Mr. Lime will pull into the driveway, press the buzzer, and wait patiently as Lime ambles down to talk through the iron bars.

In town, classmates of Lime's fifteen-year-old son, Caleb, know that the boy has his father's temperament. "Quiet and polite, but don't cross him," people say about both father and son.

Those who have lived in the area for years are also aware that Lime and the sheriff, Dan Robertson, have been best friends since high school. There are almost as many rumors about the sheriff as there are about Lime and his son.

The word among most Clarkson residents is "stay away from all three of them."

Sometimes, after a couple of beers, Mr. Lime likes to brag about his standing as "the best dog trainer in the Midwest." Sheriff Robertson sips his beer and listens patiently as Lime describes himself as a "sportsman." "If I was involved in any other sport, I'd be a rich man," Lime repeats, time and again. "People say I force these dogs to fight. Hell, I'd be hard-pressed to stop 'em."

"It's in their blood," he tells Robertson, who acts as if he's hearing this speech for the first time and not the hundredth. The sheriff laughs before finishing his beer and returning to his patrol car, saying, "It's a messed-up world, Jeremiah, that's for sure."

Caleb Lime is heir to his father's business and helps train the dogs at his father's side. Silent and brooding, the boy has a seriousness that worries his teachers and classmates, but apparently not his father.

Years ago, Caleb laughed and joked like any other child, but he's seen too much, too soon, and now he keeps his thoughts and feelings hidden. Caleb and his father lead a solitary life here. Only he, his father, and the sheriff have a key to the gate. Everyone else must press the buzzer.

One area that Mr. Lime never points out on his tours is a large patch of earth, twenty by thirty feet, where green grass never seems to grow. Hidden behind the kennel, this bare soil is turned over with a backhoe every few months, as needed. The dirt underneath this patch is the final resting place for the dogs that didn't survive their time in Lime's care.

No one is counting, especially Mr. Lime, but if they were, the remains of some forty dogs could be found in this mass grave. Dogs torn to pieces in a death match. Dogs called "punks" for refusing to fight. Dogs that came up lame and were considered not worth the time or effort to rehabilitate. Dogs that had their muzzles taped shut and were thrown into a pit with a fighting dog whipped into a frenzy by Lime.

All breeds, colors, varieties, and sizes of dogs are buried here. Apparently, they are the only living things that don't thrive in the fertile soil of Clarkson County, Indiana.

SIX

After walking half the dogs, I tell Josie I'm going to grab a late lunch, then come right back. She surprises me by handing over a five-dollar bill. "Oh, that's all right," I tell her. "My mother sets me up with a free meal."

Josie says to keep the money, then adds, "Spence, I need to talk to you about something."

Whether it's at home, school, or an animal shelter, that's never a good way to start a conversation.

I fake a smile and ask, "What's up?"

Josie fakes a smile to match mine and says, "Spence, a lot of people your age volunteer to help out around here. Most of them last a few days, maybe a week, before they get bored and split. You've been coming since early in April without missing a day."

She frowns. That's Josie, for sure, even if she's delivering good news, you're always waiting for the bad part. So I wait.

"I feel bad promising you a dog that I might not be able to deliver," she says. "What I mean is, I'm not paying you, and because of your . . . home situation, I don't think I can give you a dog either."

I'm lost. Why is she bringing this up now? To be honest, I know I can't bring a dog home to our place. It's one on a long list of "can'ts" laid down by my father: can't have friends over, can't make noise, can't stay up late on the weekends, can't watch TV—because my father chooses all the shows—can't leave a mess in any part of the house, ever, and absolutely can't have a dog.

It really doesn't matter though—pay or no pay, dog or no dog—I still like working here. It keeps me out of the house.

"Are you firing me?" I ask.

Josie laughs. "No, but I can't afford to pay you. I barely pay myself," she tells me.

"That's all right—" I start to say, but she cuts me off.

"And I won't give you a dog."

That stops me in my tracks.

"Don't you think I can take care of one?"

"Spence, I don't want a dog ending up in a house where he's not wanted. Bad things happen to these guys when they're not wanted."

"I'd protect him," I tell her.

Josie takes a long breath. "You're heading over to the diner now, right? Where your mother works?"

"Yeah," I answer, puzzled.

She stares at me. "Who protects her?"

I already know that Josie knows my mother from picking up her meals at the diner. One look at her kitchen that's mostly an office shows she doesn't do any cooking. She uses her oven for a file cabinet. Still, what Josie says next surprises me, even though it shouldn't. What I thought was our family secret is probably the kind of secret that the whole town knows about.

"Listen, Spence, you're a good worker, and I like you. That's why I'm telling you this. I know your mother, a little, from the diner. And I've heard about your father, too." She shrugs. "Lots of gossip in a small town." The look on her face tells me that whatever she's heard isn't good. How could it be?

So there it is. The secret I thought no one knew, except for the police and a few neighbors, it seems everyone knows—at least, Josie does. "So I ask you again, who protects her?"

"I try," I tell her.

"I'm sure you do," she says. "But you shouldn't have to. I'm stuck," she goes on. "I don't want to take advantage of you, but I won't send a dog home with you with the way things are." Josie lets loose another smile, a real one this time, before saying, "So, no, I'm not firing you, but . . ."

I'm tired on my way to the diner, the way I always am after something bad happens. I told Josie I'd like to stay anyway, and she agreed, then I said maybe things would be changing soon at our house, and she smiled and said she hoped that was true. While I eat, I have a hard time looking at my mother. I finish my meal quick and get up to head back to my bike. My mother asks where I'm going. "Nowhere," I say.

I don't know why I don't tell her about working at the shelter. I'm mad at her and don't know why. But I slip the five-dollar bill under my plate anyway, figuring she needs the money more than me.

For the rest of the day I don't say much to Josie either. I'm mad at her, too, without knowing why. Finally, hours later, the dogs are all walked and the day ends and I head for home.

To finally face the one person I'm really mad at.

SEVEN

Both at school and in Bent Oaks, I've got a reputation as a fighter. I deserve it, I guess, even though I usually just finish what other people start. There are a lot of trash-talkers around here, and I'm not too good at that game. My friend Miller is the champ. If you take him on verbally, he'll cut you to pieces. Of course, he's about half my size, so when he really lays into somebody, I usually end up calming the guy down—or knocking him down.

My thing is, I don't talk, I don't threaten, I just hit. Miller's a lot smarter than me, smart enough to wait until I'm around before cutting on some guy that's twice his size. I think he picked it up from his older brother, who's also smart, and a smart-ass.

I picked up my skills at home, too. Skills like how to take a hit, and how to hit back—harder.

Pedaling down the edge of the highway as the sun sets, I'm thinking about the fighting thing. When everyone around you does it, how can you get in trouble for it?

I guess I'm the answer to my own question because I've already had three suspensions this school year. My next will be my last. The principal told me, "One more infraction Mr. MacElliott and I'll see you here again next year." That's something I definitely don't want to think about.

What I am thinking about lately is prevention. I got the idea when Ms. Lepton kept repeating, "One more incident on *school property* and you are expelled."

"School property." If you're in a classroom or a hallway, riding the bus, or even standing outside waiting for the bus, you're on school property. I've got to go to class and walk the halls, but I don't have to take the bus or hang around outside the building. Now I ride my bike everywhere. If any of the guys I fought with in the past want a rematch, they'll have to catch me away from school to make it happen.

What I have planned for tonight is definitely off school property. And on a weekend.

I'm not worried about Ms. Lepton or Mr. Schmink or anyone else from the junior high. There are other details to worry about, I know, but I think I've got them all covered, like making sure Kyla stays at Loraine's, her sitter around the corner, until at least nine o'clock—and counting on my mother not to be home until then, too.

What happens tonight depends on how well I've planned things, how lucky I am, and my father.

The last time he hit my mother was two weeks ago. I was at Miller's place and when I got home our trailer was dark and my mother was in her room with the door closed. I could feel something was wrong. The place was a mess and my father was drinking and smoking in the glow of his new color TV.

The next day, sure enough, my mother was super quiet and had a swollen red cheek that she wasn't bothering to cover with makeup.

I know my father and I know he's due for another blowup any day now. That's his schedule. We all tiptoe around him when he's drunk and angry, but he also has a routine, even if he doesn't know it. Every two weeks, I'm on high alert.

I got the idea for tonight from the last time he came after me, two weeks before my mother's last beating. I didn't notice the electric tingle that night, probably because I was daydreaming on my bike ride home. But I should have.

I forgot he was around. That's when the economy first went bad and it was a new thing for my father to do his drinking at home. Before that, he hung out at Stormy's Tavern after work most nights. Good for him, and better for us.

I came speeding home from somewhere and dropped my bike against the porch before stomping up our back steps. Swinging open the back door, I was greeted with a punch to the face.

"How many times do I have to tell you not to slam your bike against the porch?" my father screamed at me.

He was drunk, drunker than usual, and looking for someone to take out his problems on.

I was lying half in and half out of the doorway, trying to clear my head from his first punch, when he picked me up by my shirt collar and pulled me inside. It was eight o'clock on a Friday night. My mother was still at work, so that left me to be that night's punching bag.

My father got in three or four good shots before I could get my hands up to defend myself. He was dragging me around the living room, shouting, "What the hell's wrong with you, anyway, Spencer?" Then he went through his usual list, landing slaps on me in between questions like, "Where the hell have you been?" and "Don't you have any homework?" and "Where's your sister and mother?"

Tough questions to answer when you're being slapped, but the correct replies would have been, "I've been hanging out with a friend," "There's no homework because it's Friday," and, "Kyla and Mom, if they have any sense, are as far away from this trailer, and you, as they can get."

But I only thought those things. I didn't say them. I didn't say anything. I knew what would happen next, but for once, I didn't care.

I just looked him in the eye and smiled.

"Nothin' to say?" was my father's only reply. That and a hard right fist that caught the left side of my face. It wasn't the sting of his punch that got to me, even though it did hurt. It was more being mad at myself for forgetting how fast he was, even dead-drunk. My only thought was to keep him from landing another clean shot on me that night, and he mostly didn't.

The next few minutes passed in slow motion as I moved backward around the couch and kitchen table with him following, throwing wild lefts and rights all the way. I was sidestepping some, blocking others, and tossing furniture in his path as we made our way around the trailer. The few punches I threw were to block his.

My father and I made three, maybe four, laps around the small space and, for the first time ever, I knew I had him.

After one more lap, he was breathing hard, then harder, and then the craziest thing happened. He sat down.

The place was trashed. He tilted a kitchen chair right side up, eased down onto it, and lit a cigarette. I stood there, waiting to see what would happen next. "Go on. Get the hell out of here," he slurred as he blew out a puff of smoke. The fight was out of him.

I walked to the bathroom and checked my face in the mirror. There were welts where the shirt had cut into my neck, some blood running from my nose and lip, and a puffy cheek. I smiled at my reflection. "Is that all you've got?" I said to the face looking back at me.

When my mother stuck her head in the front door an hour later, she gasped. Hearing my father snoring from their bedroom, she stopped in to check on me. "Are you all right?" she whispered.

"Never better," I said. "Never better."

Was it a fair fight? Nope. He was falling-down drunk and didn't know that I'd choose that night to fight back, but so what. He never fought fair when he slapped my mother or sister, or hit me with a sucker punch when I stepped through the door, or nailed me with a closed fist to the back of the head just because he'd had a bad day. But none of that mattered anymore.

The only thing that mattered was, I knew he could be beat.

I think he knew it, too.

What happened that night would eventually lead to tonight. Most people would call that a bad night, but I knew things had changed. Sitting in the dark, I thought about all the years of threats and fights and shouting, and I thought, "It's over." Not over in one night, I knew better than that, but maybe over soon if I played my cards right.

On my father's TV cop shows, things always seem to work out for the good guys—couldn't real life be like that once in a while?

A person I know gave me some advice about the law. This person told me that even if it seemed like the bad guys always got away with wife-beating and kid-beating and just about everything else, that it wasn't really true. After all, someone had to be in handcuffs in the back of all those squad cars pulling out of Bent Oaks with the sirens on and the lights flashing.

    I remembered the time we drove past the state prison in Joliet when I was ten. I couldn't believe how big it was and thought, "There must be a lot of criminals locked up in there, and they can't all be bank robbers." Even then I was hoping they had a special cell set aside for my father.

I pull up to our trailer. The station wagon's gone, but I know my mother drove it to work. Peeking inside, I can see the flickering light of the TV. Outside, it's almost dark, but still early, only eight fifteen. I roll my bike away, nice and quiet, to ride around the Oaks for a while. Tonight, the trick is to kill time until just before nine o'clock, not earlier or later.

    I look across the road to the trailer of old Mr. Moore. His kitchen lights are on and his car is parked in the carport.

    I think about Daryl, the neighborhood snoop who always seems to be hanging around our place. He's supposed to be a friend of my father's, but he sure pays a lot of attention to my mother; I bet he's got her schedule memorized. I know he'll be out on a beautiful night like this.

And Loraine is like clockwork. She'll walk Kyla back to our place at nine and talk with my mother for a few minutes before heading back home.

All possible eyewitnesses.

I ride around thinking about how things have been in the past, and how they might be in the future.

In the past, my father would hit me, or my little sister, or my mom, and no one ever said a word. People would pull their blinds and shut their doors and pretend not to hear the shouts and slaps coming from inside our trailer.

Our teachers never seemed to notice the bruises and scratches on Kyla and me. The neighbors smiled at my mother and said, "Hello, Sandy," without asking about her latest swollen lip or black eye. Later, they probably told each other we deserved it; after all, what goes on in our household is going on in lots of others, too.

Even when someone did bother to call the police, nothing ever changed.

One time, I overheard two cops on our porch calling it a "he said, she said." Meaning, even when my mother had the nerve to say, "Yes, my husband hit me," my father would lie and say she threw a pan or a dish at him and that's how the whole thing got started. "He said, she said."

In my whole life, I've seen only two people stand up to my father. One was Mr. Moore. He told my father that if he were twenty years younger, he'd "kick his ass like he deserved." My father laughed at that but not too loud, and I think I know why. Because he can't be the "he said, she said" guy with the bad wife and rotten kids if he's also the bully who punches out an old man from the neighborhood.

Behind closed doors my father can do anything he wants, but outside he has to act like good old, reasonable John MacElliott.

And even Mr. Moore doesn't push things too hard. He only calls the cops if one of us runs into the yard to escape a beating or does something else to draw attention to what's going on inside our place. I know that about Mr. Moore, even if no one else notices. If he's home—you can always tell by checking his carport for that red '71 Fairlane—and you run outside with a bloody nose or a fat lip, he'll call.

There's someone else I'm thinking of as I ride around: the new cop. I know all about the new cop, too, especially his schedule. I've watched him on patrol, rolling down the streets of Bent Oaks or cruising through Halvdale every weekend. The fact that he works Friday and Saturday nights alone in our giant trailer park tells me he's the low man on the seniority pole.

I remember his last visit to our trailer a couple of months back when he became the second guy, ever, to stand up to my father.

That night, the cop came into our living room after someone, maybe Mr. Moore, placed an emergency call. My mother was sitting at the kitchen table with a cold towel pressed to the fresh bruise on her cheek. When the cop asked to speak to my father alone, I knew he wasn't going to arrest dear old Dad. No surprise there. But what happened next surprised the heck out of me.

I watched the two of them standing almost nose-to-nose in our narrow hallway.

"You want to take a shot at me?" the cop asked calmly.

He had his hands at his sides and was staring my father straight in the eye. I couldn't believe he was challenging my father in his own house. My father used that same laugh he used on Mr. Moore but wouldn't take the bait. He just stared at his shoes. On his way out, the cop turned around and said, "Don't make me come back here tonight."

If my timing's right, the new cop will be near our place around nine o'clock, the same time my mother gets home from work and Loraine walks my sister home. With luck, Daryl will be passing by just then, and Mr. Moore will be sitting on his porch or glancing out his window. Add in anybody out for a stroll on a warm Friday night, and I've got witnesses. It's time to go home.

I hang a left, past Miller's place, and pedal up a slight grade until I can make out our trailer in the darkness. To make sure I'm not heard, I walk my bike, stopping for another peek through the kitchen window.

My father's on the couch watching one of his cop shows—beer in his left hand, cigarette in his right. I take a deep breath and open the door.

EIGHT

TC watches his mother feed and care for the dog he calls Blue. After two days, the dog is looking stronger, his eyes brighter. TC forgives him for taking food from his mother's hand but not his. "Don't you know I'm the one who saved you?" he asks.

But TC knows, or can guess, what the dog has suffered at the hands of men and gives him plenty of space.

Curious about what he saw that night in the house across the alley, TC pays a return visit. Wriggling in through the basement window, he shines his flashlight on the strange furnishings there: portable lights, a treadmill, medicines and syringes, and six bedroom doors balanced on their sides to form a fight pit.

Also blood. Lots of dried blood on the floor of the pit.

TC has heard whispers of dogfighting before; this is what it looks like. So Blue is a fighter. Well, that's no surprise. It explains the scars and the muscles, and the cars pulling out in a hurry two nights ago. It doesn't explain why Blue was left in the house alone. Or why no one has come back to claim him, yet.

Crossing back from Miss Ida's house to his mother's, TC thinks about calling the police. Then he catches himself. "Why bother?" he reasons. If wife-beating hardly counts as a crime, the mistreatment of animals will barely raise an eyebrow.

The following day, TC looks across the alley and sees two guys, cops maybe, nosing around the backyard at 730 Paxton. One guy is tall and Black, the other short and Hispanic. TC smells trouble. When he sees the men approaching his mother's house, he grabs a full garbage bag and heads for the can in the alley.

"Hey there, brother," the Black guy calls out.

All friendly-like. Too friendly to be a cop, and definitely too friendly to be on the level.

"Yeah?" TC replies warily, dropping the garbage bag into the can.

"We've been looking for our dog. He's gone missing around here a couple of days ago. Seen anything?"

"What kind of dog?" TC asks, although he knows the answer before it's given. When they describe Blue and offer a reward, TC tells the men he'll keep his eyes open, all friendly-like, and takes the slip of paper with their phone number scribbled on it.

TC knows the men will be back. From the phone in his mother's living room, he calls half a dozen animal shelters on a list he's put together. None are able to help. Most of the shelters are full, and none can promise they won't euthanize a dog that isn't adopted in seven, ten, or fourteen days.

That word, *euthanize*. It sounds so gentle, like going to sleep.

What it means is, "nobody wants to adopt a battle-scarred fighting dog, so after a week or two, we'll kill him."

Calling the men who offered the reward sounds worse. TC would rather see Blue put down than sent back to die in a fight pit.

TC is about to give up when he decides to expand his search. Tomorrow, his work shift begins at eleven a.m. If he can find a shelter within a few hours' drive, he'll take Blue in the morning before work. A shelter near Milwaukee is full, same thing for one in Indianapolis. It has to be somewhere out in the sticks.

How about this one, Pal's Place in Halvdale, Illinois? TC has to check the map to find the town. A woman on the phone says they won't euthanize, and yes, they'll take Blue if he can bring the dog and a small donation.

Taking forty dollars from underneath his mattress, TC sets his alarm for three a.m. He tells his mother that he and Blue will be leaving early, and to please pack him a meat loaf sandwich for the ride. And another for the dog. Then he goes to bed.

On the trip, too scared to look out the window at the city lights, Blue flattens to the car's backseat. At sunrise, in a rest area halfway to Halvdale, he takes a few bites of TC's sandwich and tries a tentative walk through the freshly mowed grass.

Back in the car, Blue sleeps in short spurts, his dreams interrupted by visions of the man who's held him prisoner since birth. His mother and father both belonged to the same man and lived and died on his property, a farm, where Blue was born and trained to fight. Every dog he knows shares the same kind of life there: short and violent.

Waking to a bump in the road, Blue watches TC in the rearview mirror. He senses something different in this young man—a patience in his voice and gentleness in his touch. But he has to be careful. Sometimes, the bad man switched voices to trick Blue into fighting. The man's son was kinder to the dogs than the man, but not always.

Humans have to be watched closely. A dog never knows which person might appear from day to day. The best thing to do is to wait and watch and listen.

Josie, the woman at the shelter, thinks Blue needs some peace and quiet before moving into the kennel. She sets him up in a crate in her home. Covering the crate with blankets creates a sort of cave where he can hear and smell his surroundings without the noise of other dogs frightening him.

After speaking with the woman for a few minutes, TC kneels by the crate. Reaching in, he touches Blue's paw and says goodbye. Blue thinks he is a good human and hopes to see him again. He never will.

NINE

Stepping inside, I cross to the kitchen and open the fridge. I'm not looking for leftovers. Like this morning, I'm counting the beers on the second shelf. Three.

I'm guessing my father had his first around three o'clock, at least that's his usual schedule. He's working on number nine right now, and I can tell from the way he tilts the can that it's almost empty.

I check the clock on the stove. Eight forty. My father nodded in my direction when I came in; now he's forgotten me. His cop show breaks for a commercial and he grabs the remote off the glass coffee table and switches channels.

My father's proud of his remote control. He was the first guy in the neighborhood to have one. Usually, he laughs at all the miniature cameras, video recorders, and personal computers that are starting to turn up everywhere, but he was sure interested when he heard about wireless remote controls. Imagine sitting on your couch, drinking beer, and never having to get up. Heaven.

Even with all the overdue bills piling up around our house, he couldn't resist the urge to go out and buy a useless channel switcher. That must have been some great salesman down at the appliance store because my father came home with a brand-new color TV as well.

I watch him take another pull from his beer and that reminds me of his second-favorite gadget in all the world: his can crusher.

The crusher's anchored to the kitchen wall near the fridge. Me and Kyla and my mother use it once in a while for a can of soda. Mostly, though, it's for my father's empty beer cans, of which there are plenty. Whenever he grabs a fresh beer, he pops the empty in the crusher, pushes down on the handle with a grunt, and watches as the flattened can falls into a cardboard box full of other empties.

"Dead soldiers" he calls them.

Thinking of my father's gadgets reminds me of Miller's older brother and his buddies and their newest toy. These guys are all juniors or seniors or dropouts, and last week they were out behind Miller's trailer doing their version of TV wrestling. Miller and I were watching from the road.

They had this new thing called a VHS recorder that looks like a not-too-miniature version of a real Hollywood camera. Someone had a six-pack, and they were drinking beer, slamming each other with chairs and taking turns jumping off the shed and the carport roof.

One of them balanced the camera on his shoulder while another guy crouched down behind him with a microphone. It looked like a real movie set with people timing when they would make their jumps and where they'd land.

I asked Miller where they got such expensive equipment and he said, "It fell off a truck." When I said, "Wow, really?" he just stared.

"Man, you can be so stupid sometimes," he said.

Okay, he got me on that one. His brother must have told him that they stole the camera somewhere. Now Miller knows it, and that makes him feel pretty smart. And Miller is smart, probably the smartest kid I know. But even I could see something he couldn't. These guys steal two thousand dollars' worth of brand-new camera equipment, and what do they do with it?

Sell it?

Use the money for a car, or a year of college, or to try to get out of here?

Not quite. They film themselves fighting on a stolen camera. I'm pretty sure my friend who knows about the law might call that "direct evidence of a felony." As Miller and I like to say, that is B.O.T.T.C., or Bent Oaks To The Core.

My father's moving around in the living room. I watch as he lays the remote on the glass coffee table. Getting up, he stumbles down the hallway, toward the bathroom. Coming back out a minute later, he grabs his empty beer can and walks into the kitchen. He crushes the empty before heading back to the couch with beer number ten.

I pretend to be doing my homework at the table. On his way past, he mumbles, "Why are you home?"

"I don't know," I reply, and watch as he plops back down onto the couch. It's the longest conversation we've had in weeks.

I'm still watching as he takes a pull on his fresh beer and returns his gaze to the television screen. This is it. I've got ten minutes, the amount of time until the next commercial break. Maybe less if he gets bored with the show he's watching and decides to switch channels. In my mind, I'm urging him to chug the rest of his beer. The drunker he is, the better.

Over the next ten minutes, my father takes two long drinks from the can, the cop solves his case, and the credits start to roll. I sit at the kitchen table loosening the screw that holds the wobbly leg in place, the one that broke during our last fight.

In the living room, my father feels around for his remote, but it's not in its usual spot on the coffee table. It's in my lap.

He searches, first on the floor and then the couch, feeling between the cushions and muttering under his breath. I wait. He's looking everywhere, under piles of newspapers, on both end tables, around the chair across from the couch, then he checks them all again. He's getting madder.

Now he's on his hands and knees, swearing, and using his lighter to illuminate the dark space underneath the couch.

Finally, he calls back to me, the second thing he's said since I came home tonight, "Spencer, you seen the remote?"

"I'll help you look," I reply, all helpful-like.

As my father pulls up the sofa cushions and tosses them around, I pretend to search near the kitchen. One of the tossed cushions knocks over his beer and now he's swearing louder than before. The air is buzzing with that electricity that says something bad is about to happen. Usually, that means it's time to get out. Tonight, it's exactly what I want.

He's bent over with his back turned to me, when I ask, as calm as I can, "Why can't I ever have friends over?" On his knees, searching under the couch, my father ignores me. But I won't let it go, "Or stay up late on weekends?" I ask. "Or leave my room a mess—just one time? Or watch a TV show that I want to watch?" I wait for a reaction, but there is none. "Or get a dog?" I add.

It works. My father turns to look back at me and explodes. "A dog? Jesus Christ, you pick the stupidest times to ask the stupidest questions! I'll tell you what, a dog moves in, you move out. How about that? Now help me find the damn remote."

Still on his knees, he turns to search under the old chair.

He doesn't hear as I slide the box of empties away from the kitchen wall with my foot. Asking "Is this what you're looking for?" I pull his precious rectangle of metal and plastic from my back pocket and hold it high in the air. My father climbs unsteadily to his feet.

He stares back at me, half-drunk, half-surprised, and half-relieved that I've found his little friend. That's three halves, and if that seems confusing, you should see the look on his face.

Pausing for a split second, I rear back and kick the box of empty cans as hard as I can. "What the . . . ?" he says as the empties shoot like little aluminum hockey pucks all over the room. They ricochet off the walls and furniture, and one of them flies right at my father's face. He stumbles backward, tripping over the end table and landing back in his favorite spot on the couch.

His mouth is moving but he's not saying anything as I step into the kitchen. Holding the remote in my right hand, I place it inside the jaws of the can-crusher. My father clambers to his feet and rushes me. Pretty fast for a guy on his tenth beer, but not fast enough, and he can only watch as I press down on the handle with all my might.

His little electronic marvel splinters into a hot mess of wires and plastic and cheap metal. Onscreen, the sound is deafening as the volume increases to maximum and a ghostly image flickers a beautiful bright white before the TV falls black and silent.

After that, our fight is like a repeat of our last one—except for the look in his eye. I don't recognize him anymore. Whoever this person is, grabbing my shirt and throwing wild punches, this person wants to kill me.

I have to be careful. I want to look beat up when I run into the yard, but if he gets a hold of me, I might not make it to the yard. Right at the end he does, get a hold of me, and he knocks me to the living room floor.

Quick-crawling across the carpeting, I head for the table, lying on its side half in and half out of the kitchen.

I grab at the broken leg and it comes free in my hand. Catching up, my father unleashes a hail of punches down onto my shoulders and head. Getting woozy, I can feel my whole plan slipping away. I swing the table leg to back him up and he slips on a crushed can, falling to his knees on the kitchen floor.

I climb to my feet while he claws at my legs, winded and struggling for breath from too many cigarettes. Standing above him, I raise the table leg gripped tightly in my right hand.

If I don't swing now, he'll get up. He'll get up and our life after will be exactly the same as our life before. I know that as sure as anything I've ever known. He'll win like he always does. Like all the other guys in Bent Oaks who get taken away in a squad car on a Saturday night only to turn up again on Monday morning.

Life isn't some cop show where the good guy wins and the bad guy goes to jail and everybody lives happily ever after. Life is a game where the big ones hit the little ones and get away with it because the big ones make all the rules. The kids and the stepkids and the wives and the girlfriends take the beatings, and the men sit in Stormy's Tavern complaining about their families.

Do you want a dog? Too bad because the bigger one said you can't have one.

Not because my father doesn't like dogs. I've seen him pet a neighbor's dog before. He just likes being able to say no. It makes him feel big. Hitting a woman makes him feel big. Hitting his kids makes him feel big. I don't think it makes him big, I think it makes him small.

When it's over, I stumble to the back door. Dropping the table leg, I step outside, gulping fresh air on the porch. I don't remember walking down the steps or crossing to the center of the yard, but that's where I find myself. I see Daryl lurking in the shadows of a neighbor's trailer.

He walks off without saying anything.

Across the road, Mr. Moore is reaching for the phone on his kitchen wall.

The neighborhood is quiet except for the crunch of tires on gravel as my mother pulls up in the station wagon. Seeing me standing there, my shirt half off, blood everywhere, she moves toward me, all the while searching in the darkness for my father.

The next sound I hear is the young cop turning the corner in his patrol car. As he opens his door, I hear our address, "237 Bent Oaks Drive," crackling over his police radio.

My mother takes a tissue from her purse and dabs at the corners of my mouth where the blood is already drying. Crossing to us, the cop asks, "What's going on?"

"Nothin'," I say, playing it low.

"What happened to your face?"

I just nod toward our trailer. When I turn around, I can see Mr. Moore and a couple of other neighbors watching from their windows and porches.

The cop says, "Okay, stay here," and he walks up to our front door and knocks. My mother calls out to Kyla, who's walking back home with Loraine. After a few seconds the cop knocks at our front door again, louder this time, and then walks around to the rear door, the one I came out of a few minutes earlier, and steps inside.

He's in there maybe three minutes, but it feels longer.

I see Daryl again, this time hiding in the shadow of another trailer. He won't step out into the light, and he won't come any closer. Finally, the cop comes out of our trailer, crosses to his car, and speaks into his radio: "Officer needs assistance."

Next, he calls for an ambulance before coming over and telling us to wait right there and not to go back inside. Grabbing a jacket with reflecting stripes from his back seat, he walks up the road with a flashlight to signal to the ambulance.

Later, the cop asks if we have any friends nearby. My mom points to Loraine, and the cop walks us all over to her place, tells us to stay put and that he'll be back soon.

We hang around Loraine's trailer for what feels like forever until the new cop comes back with an older cop, a sergeant, who asks my mom to step outside for a minute, and while they're standing on the porch, tells her my father is dead. I can hear them through the open window.

The sergeant sees me moving around behind the curtains. "Young man," he says, "will you join us out here, please." Looking me up and down as I step on to the porch, he asks, "You're Spencer?" I mumble, "Yes" and he pretends to be all chummy, saying, "How about I call you Spence?" I nod sure, okay, then listen as he tells the young cop to go back and watch over our trailer, warning him to "Keep people out of there and help the ambulance boys if they need it."

After the young cop walks away, the sergeant gets down to business. Sounding like he's reading from a book, he says, "Spence, Mrs. MacElliott, my condolences on your loss." Then he stares at us both. I can tell he's giving my mother time to say something polite back to him, but she's not interested. A lifetime in Bent Oaks has taught her the police don't stop by to "offer condolences."

With three of us standing on it, Loraine's porch feels pretty small. It feels even smaller when the sergeant takes a step closer, opens a little black notebook and asks, "Spencer, what transpired between you and your father tonight?" The tone of his voice tells me we're not chums anymore. "The usual thing," I say. "What thing would that be?" he wants to know. I tell him that my father was drunk, really drunk, and he started yelling and throwing things and busting up the trailer. I finish by saying, "At the end he started hitting me—but this time I fought back."

"That wasn't usual?"

"No."

After writing something in his notebook, the sergeant asks my mother if she was home during all of this. She says she got home from work and found me standing in the yard. Turning back to me, he wants me to explain how my father hit his head. When I say I don't know, he leans in farther, until he's just about breathing my air, and asks, "Spencer, did you hit your father with the broken table leg? Or any other object? If something like that happened, now is the time to tell me—I won't be able to help you later."

My mother speaks up so loud that I barely recognize her voice. "Sergeant," she tells him, "my son wasn't the one breaking up the furniture—that was my husband's habit. Last time it was the kitchen table, and it's been leaning to one side ever since. And he hit me. I tried to file a police report about it the next day, but your detective made me feel like I was wasting his time."

Almost knocking the sergeant off the porch, she swings open Loraine's front door and pushes me inside ahead of her. Turning back, she says, "I don't want to waste any more of your time either, so, if there are no more questions . . ."

Looking out the window, I can see that the sergeant's plenty mad. But what can he do? Closing his notebook, he asks my mother where we'll be staying tonight. "Right here," she says before slamming the door shut.

Getting up from the couch, Loraine walks over and slides the chain lock into its track. Meanwhile, my sister keeps her eyes fixed straight ahead, pretending to watch a comedy on TV.

TEN

It takes me a minute to figure out where I am. It's late Saturday morning, and I'm waking up on Loraine's couch. The police wouldn't let us back into our trailer last night, so we ended up sleeping here. I open one eye and see Loraine and my mother staring from the kitchen, asking how I feel. "All right," I say.

"Are you sure?" my mother wants to know.

"Can I get you something?" Loraine asks.

Is it wrong to come out and say I'm starving? I know we're not at our own place, and my father died last night, but I never had dinner, and my stomach's growling.

I don't know the rules for something like that.

But I am, starving I mean, so I say so. My mother gives me a look, but Loraine's already clattering around, grabbing bacon and eggs and bread and preserves for breakfast.

I always did sleep better at Loraine's place than at ours. Usually, those were the nights when there had been a blowup at our place or you could feel one coming. My father would be stomping around, banging drawers and cabinets, swearing, and building up to a fight. It took just a single word or look or gesture—any little thing from any of us—to light the stick of dynamite in his head.

Afterward, Loraine would offer us a safe place to stay and Kyla, my mother, and I would camp out at her trailer for a night or two. Last night was different, I suppose, but maybe not. As soon as my head hit the pillow on her couch, I was out.

I try to think about what's next. A good question. I have no idea what's next, so I decide, for now at least, not to worry about it. I only know that right now I'm hungry, so I head for the kitchen and the juice that Loraine's pouring for me.

"Thanks," I say, and ask about Kyla.

"Still asleep," my mother says.

Kyla's eleven, just two years younger than me, and totally able to take care of herself. So why does she have a sitter? For the same reason that my mother works extra shifts at the diner, and I have a place to go that no one knows about. So that none of us ever has to spend time alone with my father. A problem we won't be having anymore, I guess. It's going to take a while to get used to that. He's gone.

Last night, I snuck back and watched them take his body out to the ambulance. It was late, way past midnight, when they finally pulled out with no sirens or flashing lights. No need to hurry at that point, and they probably didn't want to wake up any more neighbors than those that were already hanging around watching. Mr. Moore was one of them. I saw him on his porch, and he gave me a nod.

From a distance, I saw Daryl and a couple of other neighbors talking with the sergeant. Their body language told me they were backing up my story—the outdoor part of it anyway.

Or maybe that's just what I wanted to think.

Watching the sergeant questioning the neighbors almost made me laugh. Mostly because, except for the young cop, none of the police who came to our trailer ever asked much of anything. Except for maybe, "Do you promise not to cause any more trouble tonight, sir? You don't want to spend the night in jail, do you?" And then they were gone—off to another house where another husband was beating another wife.

Listening to the bacon sizzling on Loraine's stovetop, I sip my juice and slip into one of my daydreams. In this one, it's summer and I'm playing with my dog. Just to make it perfect, I'm choosing an elective for freshman year because I've graduated eighth grade and Halvdale Junior High is in my rearview mirror forever.

I'm still standing there, grinning like an idiot, when Kyla joins us in the kitchen.

My sister hasn't seen me smile in a long time. And the same goes for her. Kyla used to smile and talk a lot, but she stopped doing both about six months ago and hasn't really started up again. She does now, though. Just a grin between us, but maybe that's a fresh start.

My smile disappears when I remember the sergeant telling me, "Someone will be around to talk to you in the next couple of days."

I wish I knew which "someone" that might be. A truant officer is better than a cop, and a social worker is better than either of those. But who knows? I don't know if the sergeant even knows.

Maybe I should have paid more attention to my father's cop shows. "Someone coming around to talk to you" might be one of those things they say every week right before they arrest somebody. Or maybe it means it's time for a commercial.

It's quiet while we eat, and afterward, while Kyla and I do the dishes. I don't know what my mother has in mind for the rest of the day, but I have plans.

As I head for the door, she asks, "Where are you going?"

"Home," I say.

"You can't go back in there yet, Spence."

"Why not?" I reply. "It's our house."

It's pretty clear that my mother doesn't know what to do next, and she's scared. "I need to shower and change," I tell her, and then add, "and get to work."

It's funny, the way she, Kyla, and Loraine all turn and look in my direction in the same split second. My mother opens her mouth to talk, but before she can ask where or how or when, I tell her about Pal's Place. It helps, I think, that she knows Josie from the diner. It also helps that of all the places she's been imagining I go to every day, it turns out to be an animal shelter.

But as surprised as she is, she recovers pretty quickly, saying, "Your father died last night. Show some respect."

"The dogs need me," I tell her, and I walk out the door.

Back home, our trailer looks worse but also better than I'd imagined. The cops and ambulance people moved the furniture around, probably so they could get to my father, and later, take him out.

The glass coffee table is pushed to the side, with a crack in one corner and blood on top and underneath.

The funny thing is that someone gathered up all the crushed cans and put them back in the cardboard box. They probably got tired of tripping over them and finally decided to just pick them up. Same thing with all the loose newspapers. Someone stacked them in a neat pile on the kitchen table, which is standing, barely, on three legs. The remote, or what's left of it, is still in the jaws of the can-crusher.

Mostly what I notice is the quiet. The kind of quiet that seems like it might stay that way forever, with no one charging out of a bedroom swinging a fist at you or barreling through the door all drunk and mean and swearing.

After showering, I'm getting dressed when I hear my mother and sister stepping into our trailer through the front door. I don't know what they expect to see, and honestly—aside from the blood—there've been worse nights at our house.

Kyla makes a beeline for her room and shuts the door while my mother starts cleaning up after my father for the last time. I'm heading for the back door when she says, "I'm glad you're working at the shelter. You should have told me."

"I'll tell you everything from now on," I hear myself saying, and wonder if I really mean it. "Pretty soon I'll be bringing a dog home," I add.

I watch for my mother's reaction, but there isn't one. She tells me it's okay to work today, but soon there will be a memorial service and funeral for my father.

"Whenever that is, you'll have to miss work and school for them."

I tell her I'll take a day off work if I have to, but I'm not missing a minute of school for anything or anyone, especially him. "I'm not repeating eighth grade," I say.

It's almost one in the afternoon. Most Saturdays I'm at the shelter by nine or ten. I wonder if Josie thinks I quit after our talk yesterday.

She seems surprised when I show up, but happy to see me. That makes me feel good. I don't think she's heard anything about my father, but again, maybe that's just what I want to think.

A young married couple stops by to adopt a dog and that's good too. Good for the dog and good for me.

Josie's going to show them around the kennel and introduce them to a few of the dogs. If she's heard anything, she might want to talk about it. Weekends are when people stop by to drop off or adopt dogs and it gets pretty busy sometimes. If it stays busy all day, the only ones I need to talk to are the dogs.

Speaking of dogs, I can see, barely, a new arrival in a crate covered with blankets in Josie's kitchen. While she's out showing the couple around the kennel, I sit down on the floor next to the crate. Pulling back a blanket, I see a pair of eyes staring back at me.

It's a pit bull terrier and he's big. Well, not big exactly, but muscular and covered in scars. He hangs his head like I'm there to hurt him and that makes me feel bad. "It's okay, boy," I tell him. "What's your name?" He raises his eyes to look into mine, and it feels like he wants to trust me. Or maybe I'm deciding to trust him.

I get up easy and cross to the counter where there's a jar of treats. Grabbing one, I sit back down at the crate and slide the treat through the opening. "That's for you," I tell him. Hearing the footsteps of Josie and the young couple, I pull the blankets back over the crate and disappear out the front door.

ELEVEN

Sunday, I sit around with my family.

My mother's still in shock from my father "passing away" Friday night, and so, apparently, are all the people that stop by to say how sorry they are.

I believe it. Most of them probably thought he'd leave us, or kill one of us, but they never expected him to die so young. Only thirty-six.

I sit quietly, listening to people lie about what a good man my father was and what a shame it is and blah, blah, blah. One thing I decided this weekend was to try not to lie anymore. I never was a big liar, but there are times when I know the world wants you to, like in my meeting with the principal tomorrow morning.

But I think I've figured out a way to not lie that might work. Just say nothing. So when this guy from the neighborhood keeps repeating what a great guy my father was, I just look at him. Finally, he realizes it's a one-way conversation and tells my mother he's sorry and heads for the door.

When it's quiet, I ask my uncle about building a fence to keep my dog in the yard. "You don't have a dog," he tells me.

"That's because I don't have a fence," I say, and we both laugh.

Ray lays out a long list of fence types: stockade, picket, chain-link, split rail, wrought iron. "What kind are you interested in, sport?" he asks. I tell him I'm just looking for something simple to keep my dog in the yard for the times when I can't walk him.

My uncle can fix or build anything, when he's sober. The trick is to get him started on a job early in the morning before he starts drinking. Later in the day, he starts leaning to one side and so would his fence posts, I imagine.

My mother sees the best in everyone. She knows her brother's an alcoholic. He's been one for years, but she keeps hoping he'll give it up one day. For a lot of years, she even saw the best in my father, until he was too mean for too long, and she finally gave up on him ever being a good man. Now she has high hopes for me.

Not at the present moment though. Right now, she's upset with Ray and me for joking around with all the neighbors listening. So to practice my new habit of not lying, I decide not to say anything about my dearly departed father. I just keep my mouth shut.

The rest of the day is a long wait for sundown. I never thought I'd look forward to Monday and getting back to school, but today I'm counting the hours. Finally, dinnertime rolls around. While we eat, I tell Kyla about my job at the shelter. Because of her no-talking thing it's not really a conversation, more like a monologue. She's listening though.

I tell her about the new dog kept in a separate cage in Josie's kitchen, a tough-looking pit bull that someone rescued from a dogfighter in Chicago. Hearing that, my mother says to "be careful." Ray's opinion is "Devil dog. Better keep away from that one." Kyla surprises me by speaking up. "I think you should be his friend," she says.

"Maybe I will," I reply, "maybe I will."

TWELVE

I'm watching Mr. Schmink read my essay.

And he really reads it. Like it's not something I knocked out in twenty minutes, but some masterpiece that I worked on for hours. That's what I like about Mr. Schmink, but also what drives me crazy: things really matter to him.

Another thing I like: he hasn't mentioned my father. Except for when I showed up in his office and he turned white as a ghost and said, "Spencer, I didn't expect to see you today," which meant, "I heard what happened this weekend and I never thought you'd be here this morning."

"We have an appointment, remember?" I said, pretending to be calm.

The truth is, if I hadn't shown up today, the principal would've expelled me and I'd be repeating eighth grade—and these conversations with Mr. Schmink—next year.

After he calmed down, Mr. Schmink asked, "Anything you want to talk about?" That was code for "Do you want to tell me what happened?" Which I could answer one of two ways.

One, I could say no. Or, two, I could blurt out a confession like a suspect on one of my father's cop shows.

I chose one.

Now Mr. Schmink's back to reading. He's even making little notes in the margins. I watch him for a while, then look around his office at his kid's artwork hanging all over the place.

The essay is only part of my "readmittance" to Halvdale Junior High. The rest is a meeting with Ms. Lepton—about ten minutes from now. Mr. Schmink looks over his glasses at me and it makes me feel like this essay matters somehow.

My father never looked at a single thing I did for school, from kindergarten right up through eighth grade, not once.

Watching Mr. Schmink read, I'm wishing I'd put more time into writing the thing. But I guess it's too late for that. While he's finishing up, I'm thinking about this girl Alicia, who's in two of my classes, three if you count lunch. Would it be too bold to sit at her lunch table my first day back?

I can't eat with Miller. He's got a different lunch period. Except for my usual table of misfits from Bent Oaks, I've got nowhere else to sit. Something tells me if I don't start breaking away from the Oaks crowd pretty soon, I never will. And it's not like anyone else is holding a place for me. I decide to see how the morning goes and figure it out later.

I guess I've been daydreaming again because Mr. Schmink's calling my name and holding my essay like it's something he pulled out of the trash. "How is it?" I ask.

"Fair," he says. "Disregarding the spelling errors, and the fact that you spent, what, half an hour on it yesterday afternoon?"

"Twenty minutes," I say. "Friday morning. The last day of my suspension."

Mr. Schmink gives me a look, and already I feel bad about my answer. Before I can come up with a better one, he looks at the clock, says, "Uh-oh!" and pushes me out of his office door and into the hallway. We half walk and half run toward Ms. Lepton's office.

Waving my essay as we go, Mr. Schmink says, "Now, here's what I want for your next one."

I'm surprised because I didn't know these essays were going to be a regular thing.

Mr. Schmink looks me in the eye like he knows I'm surprised but doesn't care, and then he really burrows in. "Spence, I want you to be more specific about these fights you've been in. You didn't just 'get into trouble.' You started fistfights with three other students in three other incidents, that we know of. And it's not because 'everyone around here does it.' I want you to think about that, and what causes these . . . situations, and about what you can do to change things. Got it?"

Just out of sight of the principal's office, Mr. Schmink pulls me close to the wall.

Leaning in like he's kind of tired, he says, "Listen, Spencer, you're right on the fence around here, and if you're not willing to help yourself, there's only so much I can do for you."

First period is starting soon and people are stopping to point and whisper. We must make quite a sight, the killer kid and the guidance counselor, huddling outside Ms. Lepton's office. I'm nodding okay and turning to head inside when Mr. Schmink grabs me by the elbow and says, "One more thing you can write about is why you think you can handle the responsibility of a dog. Oh, and also why you say you like most dogs better than most people. Okay? Great."

As Mr. Schmink turns to walk in ahead of me, I wonder whose side he's on in this situation. Then I remember that he was the only one standing up for me after my last fight. I guess I really let him down with my twenty-minute essay.

I decide to write like the Hemingway of essays next time to thank him for helping me—if there is a next time.

It's funny, but maybe the whole thing with my father will help me out today. I mean, the principal's not exactly going to worry about one more kid getting into one more fight when that same kid might be going away to juvenile hall soon. Or worse. Dying might be the only favor my father ever did for me.

Turning the corner, I see Ms. Lepton talking to her secretary.

She sees me too, and looks even more shocked than Mr. Schmink did earlier.

Walking in ahead of me, Mr. Schmink says, "Good morning, ladies."

The secretary smiles and says hello. Ignoring Mr. Schmink completely, Ms. Lepton zeroes in on me. "Does your mother know you're here, Spencer?"

"Yes, ma'am," I say. "It's a school day."

I said I wouldn't lie anymore and, technically, I'm not. My mother knows I'm here all right. She wanted me to stay home, to mourn I guess, and after ten minutes of yelling back and forth about "respect for the dead" and "what will people think," I finally just grabbed my essay and jumped on my bike.

Kids are supposed to be in school on school days, right? Well, here I am.

I can see Ms. Lepton thinking. There's fourteen more days of school this year spread out over the next three weeks. If she suspends or expels me today, we have to start all over again together next fall. Or, she can readmit me to class, which was the point of this meeting anyway, and hope that I make it through the rest of the year with no more problems. If we're both lucky, we'll never see each other again.

My mother's always telling me to start thinking like an adult. I think I just did.

I look from the principal to Mr. Schmink. I never really thought about it before, but Ms. Lepton's his boss. That can't be too easy to deal with. I wish I could take him with me to Halvdale High next year, if I make it.

    With a shrug, Ms. Lepton tells her secretary to hold her calls. Then she tells Mr. Schmink and me to follow her into her office. Walking in, I realize I have absolutely no idea what's going to happen, no idea at all.

THIRTEEN

Mr. Lime has so many dogs now that he schedules fights twice a month. Whether at home in Indiana or on the road in Chicago or Memphis, he makes nearly as much money from his "hobby" as he does from farming.

His son, Caleb, attends high school, farms the land, and helps to train his father's dogs until the sun sets and the moon rises in the sky. His father shows him the large stacks of bills in their safe, telling him it will all be his one day.

The money barely interests Caleb. What he really wants is a good night's sleep.

Lime has lots of dogs, thirteen in fact, but one is missing.

This isn't a case of a heartbroken dog owner searching high and low for a lost pet. This is business. Spike is one of Lime's top dogs, and he wants him back. The sooner he returns, the sooner he can begin earning money again.

At their last fight in Chicago, half a dozen men and over a dozen dogs were packed into the cellar on Paxton Avenue when a fight broke out.

A human fight.

One man, drunk and unhappy, demanded his money back after one of his dogs had lost an earlier fight. Grumbling that he'd been cheated, the man told anyone who would listen that he would get even. No one paid much attention until he pulled out a gun and began waving it around the crowded basement.

Lime had set up the evening's fights with two Chicago "associates," Carl Washington and Javier Rodriguez.

Carl and Javi find vacant houses for the fights, invite other dogfighters, and help Lime manage the five or six dogs he usually brings along on fight nights.

Carl Washington is tall and Black, Javier Rodriguez is short and brown, and Jeremiah Lime is a stocky white man of average height. They share one characteristic, however, in that they all look "shady." Seeing them on the street, a passerby might think that, together, they resemble a multicolored, small, medium, and large picture of bad deeds.

Carl is a gambler, and Javi an addict and thief who can, usually, be counted on to back Lime up when things get rough. But a drunk man waving a gun in a confined space changes all the usual rules.

When the man produced a weapon, Javi ran for the stairs while Carl ducked behind another dogfighter. Lime himself had to hit the gunslinger over the head with a bottle. Two shots went off during the struggle. After that, someone thought they heard the wail of a police siren and everyone scattered for their cars.

Deciding that it was time to go, Lime, Carl, and Javi gathered up five of Lime's dogs and escaped in three vehicles, with the plan to meet up later.

Cowering in the pit, Spike saw his chance. He crawled around the water heater to a narrow space behind the furnace and stayed there for three hours, until the only sound in the old house was his own breathing. That night, and the next day, Lime had called Javi and Carl nonstop from Indiana, but got no reply. Cursing, he slammed his telephone into its cradle, cracking the kitchen drywall in the process.

When Spike finally ventured out from his hiding place in the now quiet house, he didn't know what to expect. Working his way upstairs, he thought he might taste freedom for the first time in his life.

In a strange way, he was almost relieved when he scratched at the closed front door. What would he do out there? Where would he go?

Shuddering at the thought of Mr. Lime coming back to collect him, Spike began the first of many tours around the house, searching for a way out. For two days, he walked the hallway, tracing his steps from room to room, hoping to locate an escape route. Later, he began to hope that Lime would return and bring along a few sips of water and scraps of food.

Lime continued calling Chicago. He had no way of knowing that Carl was spending the next two days as "a guest of the county" at the Cook County Jail. Picked up for a parole violation, Carl was allowed just one phone call. He dialed Javier.

Deep into a drug binge, Javi promised to check the house on Paxton Avenue later that night. He even wrote himself a note on the back of a fast-food receipt. Javi then folded the note neatly and placed it in his wallet, never to be seen again.

And so it was simply luck that brought Michael and TC to Miss Ida's place before Lime or one of his helpers.

Luck that they arrived that night, because the following morning might have been too late.

Luck that TC's mother had heard a "baby crying."

A dog's life is based on luck: good and bad. Spike had waited three years for one lucky night. Mr. Lime cursed his bad luck and vowed to get his dog back.

FOURTEEN

Sometimes it's easier to be the person everyone's talking about than the people doing the talking. It's like no one knows what to say to me. Whenever I catch someone looking in my direction, they look away.

I'm sitting in the lunchroom with my day half over and thinking about my meeting with the principal yesterday morning.

While I sat squirming in my seat, Ms. Lepton called someone at the district and told him about my situation. Then she did a lot of listening to the voice on the other end of the line. Afterward, she turned to me and said, "I have no legal basis to keep you out of school, so you may resume classes."

Wow, nice to see you too.

As Mr. Schmink and I made our way back down the hall, he warned me "to keep my nose clean."

I didn't need to be told, but it never hurts to be reminded. So, I knew what I had to do: stay out of trouble from that moment until the end of the school year.

Because of the meeting, I was late to my first class. When I came in, the room got quiet. Everyone stared as I made my way to my seat. My teacher, Mrs. Delaney, waited while I sat down, and for the rest of the period people kept turning around for a look at the two-headed monster that is me.

Between periods was worse. A couple of times I almost looked to see what everyone was staring at until I remembered it was, oh yeah, me again.

Gym was okay: shooting baskets with Miller and a couple of other guys while Coach read a newspaper and pretended to be doing his job. Mostly, the day passed in a daze, but I made it through, went to work at the shelter, crossed one day off my calendar, and now I'm back again.

That brings me to lunch today. I grab a tray, load it up, walk past the Bent Oaks crew, and plop down at the far end of Alicia's table. She turns and gives me a smile. Just a smile, but right now that feels like a lot.

I know I'll catch some grief later for ignoring the guys from the Oaks, but the last thing I feel like doing is talking about my father. Besides, those guys have enough Bent Oaks stories to keep them talking for a whole lot of lunch periods. I take Alicia's smile as a sign. A sign that I have at least one possible friend around here.

When I look back from Alicia, I notice that I'm sitting across from Olsen. Olsen's this shy, skinny kid that a lot of the guys from the Oaks table have picked on in the past. I'm glad I'm not one of them; still it's kind of awkward.

I give Olsen a grin, and he gives me a look that says, "Why in the hell are you sitting here?"

"Is that the roast beef?" I ask, studying the mystery meat on his tray.

"Supposed to be," he says. "Do you want some?"

"No thanks," I laugh, before offering a breaded something that might once have lived in the sea. "Fish stick?"

Olsen makes a face. "I'll stick with the beef."

After that we get along all right, and I figure I'll sit with him for the rest of the week. So, Olsen's talking to me, and Alicia's smiling, and that makes two possible friends. A start.

Blue makes three. He's the pit bull that belongs to the pair of eyes I saw the other day at the shelter. Technically, Blue can't talk, but he's a pretty good listener. Yesterday, after finishing my shift, I sat outside his cage and read my assignments out loud to him. The most amazing part of that story is, I actually did my homework.

Blue ended up here when this guy from Chicago found him locked inside a dogfighting house. When he called animal control, they told him he'd be put down within a week. Blue's pretty scarred from fighting, and, honestly, most people that stop by a shelter are looking for a puppy to adopt. So the guy called around. He found Josie's number somewhere, called her up, and now Blue's living at Pal's Place.

Josie says Blue's putting on weight and getting his strength back, but he still has a long way to go.

When he got here you could see his ribs right through his skin. He's still pretty nervous around people and other dogs. Yesterday, I walked him for the first time. We did all right until a car roared past on Quentin Road and he pulled me off into the weeds. But he settled down right away afterward. A good sign, I think.

I can't figure out what kind of messed-up people get their kicks watching two dogs fighting.

Probably the same kind who gather around and cheer whenever a fight breaks out in Bent Oaks.

I mean, I get in my share of fights, but at least I'm in there hitting or getting hit. I'm not watching two other guys tear each other to pieces for entertainment.

Thinking of messed-up people reminds me of Josie. Okay, that came out wrong. I mean, *she's* not, but she's tired of dealing with people who are. She really loves animals, and she's seen too many people hurt them, and I guess, one day she finally ran out of patience.

She told me how one morning last week she noticed something strange out by her front gate. When she went to have a look, she found a dead dog tied to the fence.

"Why would they tie him up if he was dead?" I asked. I could almost hear Miller wondering if I'll ever get tired of asking dumb questions.

"He wasn't dead when they left him," she said. "They probably hit him with their car and found a piece of rope and left him here, figuring we'd find him in the morning and nurse him back to health. They didn't bother to take him to a vet or ring the doorbell or beep their horn. Nothing."

Yesterday, Josie told me we're getting a pit bull mother and six pups this weekend. We've already got twenty-eight dogs at the shelter. Seven more will make thirty-five in a place that's licensed for twenty.

Josie said if the neighbors didn't complain, she'd keep a hundred dogs at her place. I think she would, too, if she could afford it.

In Josie's opinion, most people don't care about strays in or out of a shelter. Most of these dogs are born into bad luck and live and die the same way. The only time most people even notice a stray is if they hit it with their car or see one starving by the side of the road. Then they're all like, "This is terrible. Someone should do something."

Before they get back into their car and go out to dinner.

Working at the shelter makes me feel like I'm doing something good. After all the years of not-so-good things at the Oaks, it feels, I don't know, important.

I know I could help out by taking home one of the shelter dogs, but, so far, I haven't found the right one. Blue might be a good choice, but I'm not sure he knows how to act around people, and, to be honest, his looks might scare my mother and sister. Besides, Ray and I still have to put up the fence, so I'm on Raytime on that one.

After work today I think I'll bike over to the ice cream place in Halvdale where Alicia works part-time. I thought I'd stop in and get a cone and leave. Bad idea? Maybe I'll come up with something better while I'm out walking the dogs this afternoon.

Speaking of ideas, I got a good one from the cop that showed up at our trailer the night my father died. He had these stripes on his jacket that reflect a car's headlights. I picked some up at the hardware store and put them on my bike for all the night riding I've been doing lately. Geeky but effective.

Believe me, the same people who would hit a dog on a dark country road would run over a kid on a bike, too. Anyway, no one knows it's me in the dark. They only see the stripes, and I get to where I'm going alive.

It's too bad all the stray dogs can't be hooked up with reflectors. They might live longer. But I guess if anyone bothered to stop and put a reflective collar on them, they might just as well take them home and then they wouldn't be strays anymore.

At the ice cream place, Alicia's busy with another customer, so I order a cone from her coworker and head back out to my bike. That turned out all right, since I hadn't planned what to say and instead we just smiled at each other. Biking through town, I slurp my cone while I pedal.

Back home, my mother hits me with the news that my father's memorial service will be Thursday afternoon, the day before my birthday.

I tell her that I absolutely, positively, won't miss a minute of school for anyone, especially my father. She tells me to calm down, that she's already thought of that, and that I can come over right after school. For once, we're not arguing.

As we're standing there not arguing, I hear a knock at the door. Looking out, I see the sergeant, the older cop from last Friday night. I open the door slowly. He asks if my mother's home, and when he sees her, basically invites himself inside, ignoring me.

"Mrs. MacElliott," the cop says, "how are you?" My mother says she's fine but not much more and waits to hear whatever bad news he's there to deliver. The news is that the local judge is holding an "informal inquest" Saturday morning. He wants me to be there. "Just to clear up some details."

When my mother asks if we have to attend the hearing, the sergeant says no, he doesn't believe we are "compelled to attend," but it would be in "our best interest" to do so. "It's better than getting a subpoena to attend a formal hearing later." He says the last part like he wouldn't mind dropping a subpoena on me one little bit.

    Watching from the couch, my sister's studying the sergeant. She's wearing a look that says she wouldn't mind showing him to the door, and slamming it shut behind him. Neither would I, Kyla, not one little bit.

FIFTEEN

I'm struggling to tie my tie for the memorial service.

I can't remember ever seeing my father in a tie, and I guess he never saw me in one either. I want to tell my mother, why bother? No one but a couple of my father's barroom buddies is going to show up. But I keep my mouth shut and that turns out to be a smart move.

A few of my father's pals from Stormy's Tavern do show up, but don't stay very long. And a couple of his coworkers from the foundry stop by, too, but that's not who fills up the funeral home. Mostly, it's friends of my mother's from all over town that pack the place.

Since he was down to part-time, my father really didn't see his work friends much anymore. As far as his drinking buddies, the one way he tried to save money was by doing his drinking at home and not down at Stormy's. All in all, I think a lot of his old pals just kind of forgot about him.

But my mother, that's a different story. I think she knows everyone in town. Most of them stay and talk, then leave behind a big plate of food of one kind or another before they go.

It takes Ray and me two trips in the car to get it all home.

I guess when someone dies, people think the rest of the family will starve or something. That would make sense if anything happened to my mother, but it's not like my father ever cooked a meal in his life.

We'll probably have lots of extra food around the house from now on—extra beer anyway. I'm thinking of the two cans my father left behind. They'll be in our refrigerator for a long time. Unless Ray drinks them.

Miller shows up wearing a tucked-in white shirt. Miller wears a white shirt about as often as I wear a tie. Someone should take a picture. It's cool of him to come since my father never wanted him hanging around our place.

Total honesty? My father never wanted any of my friends, or Kyla's, hanging around our place.

Another one of his rules.

Mostly, there are a lot of ladies coming up to me and saying things like, "I'm an old friend of your mother's and I just wanted to say how sorry I am." Then they get real quiet. After that, they give me "the look." The look that says they'd love to know what happened that night, but, of course, they'd never ask.

So, instead, they just stand there politely and wait.

They'll be waiting a long time.

I'm in another one of my trances, staring off into the distance and wondering why everyone talks about only that one night. Why not all the other nights? The nights when my father shouted and yelled and beat his wife and kids, while all the people who knew about it never said a word. I should ask them, "What happened? If you love my mother so much, why didn't you do anything?"

Another one of my father's rules: kids answer questions, not ask them.

When I look around, the ladies have moved on. I'm standing all alone in the middle of the "Bereavement Room."

I'm thinking about this person again, the one who knows about the law. I asked what an inquest is, even an "informal" one. The answer: it's to determine cause of death. To decide if someone died from natural causes or suicide or an accident or murder.

Maybe, after Saturday, I'll have an answer for everyone's questions. Especially, if the judge finds my father's cause of death to be accidental.

Back home after the service, I'm taking off the suit that I borrowed from my uncle. I guess Ray wore it when he was sixteen, and now it fits me and I'm only thirteen. I ask my mother if I should return it and she says, "You better keep it awhile. You might need it."

That's her way of saying, "You might want to wear it to the inquest Saturday, and if that's a fail, save it for the trial."

That's because I told her something else I learned about the inquest. My friend said that if a judge decides my father's death is "suspicious," he can order a full murder investigation. An investigation could lead to a trial. If that happens, it's going to take a lot more than Ray's old suit to help me out.

Grabbing a hanger, I carry the suit out to the hall closet. In the kitchen, Ray's pouring whiskey from a flask into his coffee cup. Kyla's on the couch watching TV.

Opening the closet, I glance at the top shelf. There, in an old shoebox, sits what's left of my father's remote control. I stashed it out of reach until I can get around to throwing it out. It's funny that in all the questions about that night, no one ever asked me about the remote. I could tell them quite a story. But maybe I better keep that to myself for a while.

I hear my mother's voice. Looking around, I see her in the kitchen, motioning me over. I study her face to see how she's doing. At the service, she was crying, then laughing with some old friends, then crying again. I wait to see which version of her is sitting in our kitchen.

Ray says, "Take care of that suit, sport, I plan on losing a lot of weight soon." That's funny. Mostly because Ray already looks like a skeleton. Everyone laughs, so it seems like maybe we're all good.

My mother clears her throat and says, "I want to talk to you about something."

There's that phrase again. I smile and wait.

She tells me that she hasn't forgotten my birthday and that she and Ray want to give me my present now: Ray's going to help me build the fence for our backyard, and she's going to pay for all the materials. Up until now, I haven't officially heard I could get a dog, so this is big news.

I thank them both before high-fiving Kyla on my way back to my room. Honestly, another birthday doesn't mean anything to me. Today I'm thirteen, in a few days I'll be fourteen. I'm not expecting much of a difference.

But the fence, that's sweet.

Thinking about birthdays reminds me of something though. Something that's been nagging at me for a while, and I think I'm finally starting to figure it out. It's the idea of showing up at Halvdale High next fall, if I make it, with a reputation as a fighter.

I'll be a fourteen-year-old with a bunch of seventeen-year-olds lining up to kick my ass. That's definitely something to not look forward to, unless I change my ways.

Grabbing a clean towel, I head for the bathroom. Aside from dog walking, showering is when I do my best thinking. Right now, there's way too much to think about. I hop in the shower with my head practically spinning.

So far I've knocked off four days of school with no fights and no problems. I was right about one thing: in a strange way my father's death has bought me some time. My teachers have all been super nice to me, and everyone else is sort of hanging back and watching. That might last a few more days, but if it gets me closer to graduation day, I'll take it.

Now I've got a date with a judge next Saturday. If I make it through that, maybe I can start thinking about bringing home a dog, and, after that, summer school. Then there's Alicia. Has anyone from Bent Oaks ever dated anyone from Halvdale? Not that I can remember. Also, I'm planning on pushing my mother to get us out of the Oaks sometime soon. Is this summer too soon? Even moving to the outskirts of Halvdale might be a nice first step.

So many thoughts about so many things that I swear the bathtub's starting to spin. To calm down, I practice a trick Mr. Schmink taught me: deep breathing. In through the nose, out through the lips. I spit out a mouthful of water and decide to try it again later, out of the shower.

Toweling off, I wonder if all my plans are possible, if any of them are possible. Getting past the inquest, making it through two more weeks of school, bringing home a dog, surviving summer school, seeing more of Alicia, getting out of Bent Oaks . . .

I don't remember going back to my room or climbing into bed, but I must have because the next thing I know it's Friday morning and my alarm pulls me from a deep sleep.

SIXTEEN

Spike is adjusting to life at the shelter and his new name. The woman calls him Blue and brings food and water and carries the smell of other dogs and other places. Everything seems different here. Different and new, and he waits for things to turn bad and violent like they were on the farm, but so far they haven't and good things seem possible.

Every afternoon, a boy comes and calls him by his new name and takes him for walks. Sometimes, the boy sits outside his crate and talks to him after their walks and Blue begins to trust him.

The boy here looks a little like the boy from the farm. That boy sometimes looked at him gently or spoke softly, but only sometimes. Until the bad man came around and Blue could smell fear on the boy. He watched as the boy's shoulders stiffened and his voice grew sharp.

On the farm, there were only two people, the boy and the man. Now Blue is seeing more people, and he has to learn to tell whether they are good or bad. As a puppy, he thought all people were good. Later, he thought they were all bad. Like the men who helped out the man at the farm. Or the men at the dogfights who prodded and jeered and laughed.

Now it seems that some people are good and some are bad, and you can't tell by looking. That's the hard part.

Dogs see people in shades of gray—from light gray to dark gray and all the variations in between. Some good people are dark gray and some are light gray. Like the young man who saved Blue from the house and brought him to the shelter. He was dark gray and so was his mother, and Blue trusted them. The woman and the boy here are light gray, and Blue trusts them too.

The man on the farm is the lightest gray of all and the cruelest. Blue guesses that the shade of gray doesn't matter, that there must be some other way to tell good people from bad people. Maybe you just have to get to know them to tell which is which.

Blue wants to warn the people here, the woman and the boy, about the light gray man who kept him prisoner on the farm for his entire life. That man still appears in Blue's dreams. It's why he whimpers in the night and sometimes sounds like a crying baby.

Blue knows that the man will follow him and try to bring him back to the farm. No one can stop him. He's the alpha in every pack that Blue has ever seen him in, and the dogs all fear him and give in to his power.

He hopes that if the man comes to take him, he'll be lucky again. Dogs know about luck. If they're lucky, they live a good life with a loving owner, playing in a yard and running with children and sleeping on a couch between two light or dark gray people and growing old along with those same children.

If they're not, well, most are not, and Blue doesn't want to think about bad luck at a time like this.

Right now, Blue considers himself very lucky. He's getting stronger every day. Maybe soon he'll be allowed into the building along with the other dogs that he smells nearby and can hear throughout the day. Then he can tell the other dogs about the cruel man and maybe, somehow, they can warn the woman and the boy.

Until then, he'll do what he's always done, what dogs have done since they first shared a cave with humans—wait and watch and listen.

SEVENTEEN

I'm the mad biker of Halvdale. I pedal to and from school, out to Pal's Place, over to the diner, and sometimes across town to Alicia's ice cream shop. I heard of this bicycle race in Europe called the Tour of France that no American has ever competed in.

Maybe I'll be the first.

I'm riding home from the shelter thinking about Alicia. Today, I mentioned it was my birthday and she said, "You should have told me!" Then she ducked back in the lunch line and got me a big piece of chocolate cake.

Later, when I shared my birthday news with Josie, she reached in her pocket and handed me ten dollars. Now I'm wondering who else I can tell.

Just to make sure I'm not imagining the whole thing, I stand on my pedals and feel in my jeans for the two five-dollar bills. Still there.

Zoning out on these bike rides makes the ride go faster. But this time I've zoned out about a half mile past the Oaks. When I finally get home, I almost hit my uncle. He's bent over in our yard, pulling a tarp over a pile of fence posts, wire, hammers, nails, a post-hole digger—everything we need to build our fence. Ray came through for me! And he's coming back Sunday to start on the fence.

If I survive the inquest on Saturday.

Walking inside, I smell my favorite meal cooking: roast chicken. I notice a chocolate cake on the counter, which I'm guessing I wasn't supposed to see because my mom shouts, "Oh, Spence!" Then she calls Kyla, hands her the cake, and turns to block my view while my sister disappears down the hallway.

"You're home early," my mother says, all nonchalantly. I tell her it's six thirty, my usual time getting home from the shelter. "There's something for you in the yard. Did you see it?"

"How could I miss it," I reply.

Turning back to her cooking, she says, "I'm afraid that's all I got you, except for your favorite meal."

I turn around, expecting to see my uncle following me through the open door, but he's walking off toward home. I'm about to call after him when my mother says to let him go.

"Something's bothering him lately," she says. "I'll talk to him Sunday."

After dinner, I'm sitting on the couch eating a piece of chocolate cake, my second today, and thinking about my uncle. He doesn't look good lately. And something's bothering him, that's for sure. It can't be my father dying since the two of them never really got along. Maybe working with me on the fence Sunday will help—it's got to be better than sitting in some dark tavern, drinking and smoking.

Leafing through a dog-training book, my gift from Kyla, I'm thinking about tomorrow's talk with a judge. I hope he hasn't heard about my birthday, figuring he's more likely to sentence a fourteen-year-old to juvenile hall than a thirteen-year-old. But maybe that's just my imagination.

Getting up from the couch, I head for the kitchen and another slice of cake—just in case wherever I end up doesn't serve dessert.

EIGHTEEN

Everyone wants to know what happened that night. The cops, the neighbors, kids at school, even people I've never met before. Everyone wants to know, but no one asks. Except for the judge. He just asked for the second time.

Leaning across his desk, he shoots me a big, fake-friendly grin and says, "Young man, just stick to the facts and tell the truth and everything will turn out just fine."

"Just fine," I think. Now I'm the one grinning, almost.

We're at the informal inquest, which sounds kind of friendly except that it's one step before an actual coroner's inquest, which is one step before an actual murder trial, where the actual defendant would be me. So maybe not so friendly, after all.

The main reason we're all here is that no one knows if my father hit his head on a glass coffee table and died, or if someone else, me, for example, bashed his head in with a "blunt object."

Also, the fact that I'm fourteen has everyone kind of messed up.

The judge starts out by saying not to be fooled, that just because it's a Saturday and we're in his office, not a courtroom, this is still an "official proceeding." Then he asks me a few "warm-up questions."

"School?"

"Halvdale Junior High."

"Are you currently suspended for fighting?"

"No, sir."

"No, you're not?"

"No, that was last week."

And so on. Really, the judge doesn't have to ask a lot of questions—all he has to do is read the reports. My family's in a lot of reports: police reports, emergency room reports, social worker reports, and, lately, lots of "official letters" from the principal to my mother. One time I even wrote a report for Mrs. Delaney's class about all our other reports, but I bailed at the last minute and didn't turn it in.

The judge takes a sip from a can of Mello Yello and rubs his stomach. I almost feel bad for making him come to work on a Saturday. He's in a suit, not his robes, and the six people here are all waiting for me to talk, "officially." I look from the judge to my mother to the cop who came by our trailer that night to the social worker to the court reporter to the bailiff. The bailiff takes over.

"Name?"

"Spencer T. MacElliott."

"Date of birth?"

"May twenty-fifth, 1965."

"Address?"

"Bent Oaks Trailer Park, number 237."

"Do you swear to tell the truth, the whole truth, and nothing but the truth, so help you God?"

"Uh-huh."

"What's that?"

"I do."

"All right, be seated."

All that time with my left hand on the Bible, like nobody ever lied while holding one before. It's quiet. If you listen hard enough, I swear you could hear a pin drop. What I hear, for some strange reason, is my uncle's voice.

I remember Ray telling me once, "Be careful what you say, and who you say it to." He was talking about the government, I think, but it might have been about school, or the rich versus the poor, or even life in Bent Oaks.

My uncle's like a river. You have to jump in and swim along for a while, then jump out before the current pulls you under. One true thing he told me at the memorial service was "Strange how none of these people ever cared about our family before."

I try to remember: Who were my friends before, and who will be my friends after?

The person who tells me about the law told me something else interesting: that I can't be forced to testify against myself. Not at an informal hearing like today's or a coroner's inquest or even a trial. It's called my right against self-incrimination. This person told me not to help the cops by talking too much. If I do, they might charge me with my father's murder. The point is, why help them put me in jail?

I share this news with the judge and watch as the fake grin falls right off his face. He sits there thinking for a minute before asking, "And who told you about this aspect of the law—I assume you didn't hear it on the schoolyard?"

I want to say, "I saw it on one of my father's cop shows." Instead, I tell the truth, sort of, "Just a friend, your honor, I don't want to say who."

The judge laughs a little before asking, "Is this nameless person a lawyer?"

"No, sir"

"Well, your friend is right," he says, "you cannot be compelled to testify at this, or any other hearing. But you can be compelled to attend another, more formal hearing, which I am going to schedule right now."

Staring right at me, the judge says, "Since we're not getting anywhere today, we'll do things proper. Case is referred to docket for a full coroner's inquest in two weeks' time." Then he barks at the bailiff to tell Mr. Moore and any other witnesses waiting in the hall to go on home. Checking his calendar, he says: "Inquest date: Monday, June eleventh, 1979, at nine thirty a.m. Hopefully, I'll have a copy of the coroner's report by then."

I fidget in my chair, but the judge isn't finished yet. He looks at the social worker and asks, "Ms. Fenneman, should the witness be held over at the juvenile detention center until that time?" Ms. Fenneman's been out to our house half a dozen times—I know her like a sick kid knows the school nurse. She's got a file with my name on it sitting on the desk in front of her. After flipping through the file for a minute, she clears her throat and says, "I don't believe the witness is a flight risk, or a risk to the community, your honor. And there is the matter of completing the current school year."

Turning back to me, the judge says, "I'm accepting the social worker's recommendation and granting you a conditional release until the inquest. Break any of the provisions of that release and I'll have you picked up and taken to juvenile hall. Do you understand?"

"Yes, sir," I gulp.

"Don't you want to hear the provisions first, you may not like them." I nod yes and the judge tells me to "Keep my voice up." Then he rattles off a list of rules: "Attend school every day from first bell to last bell—no legal troubles of any kind, truancy, fighting, whatever. Continue volunteering at the animal shelter at least four days a week. And do not leave the county. Do you understand and accept these conditions?"

I gulp out another "Yes" and the judge says, "So recorded."

The court reporter has been typing away like a madwoman during all of this. She's still trying to catch up when the judge pounds his desk with a little wooden hammer; he rises from his seat while the bailiff motions for everyone else to stand. Sipping the last of his soda, he watches as we all file out of his office.

    My mother and I follow the bailiff down a long, curved hallway. I wonder where we're headed until I see a square of sunlight shining through the frosted glass of a side door. The bailiff unlocks the door and I step out into the parking lot—and freedom—for the next couple of weeks anyway.

    Across the lot, our station wagon sits all alone under a chestnut tree. My mother starts the car and drives, quiet and glassy-eyed, just staring out the window at the passing scenery. It's the same scenery she's seen her whole life, so you'd think she'd have it memorized by now, and I don't think she even notices as the run-down houses of town give way to the small farms, rusty warehouses, and smelly factories that lead back, eventually, to Bent Oaks.

NINETEEN

Can you be asleep, know you're asleep, and want to wake up but can't? I'm tossing and turning with every thought that's been banging around in my head for the past week: coroner's inquest, Ms. Lepton, the judge, the cops from the night my father died, and some dogfighter whose face I can't make out.

They're all trying to stop me from leaving the Oaks and getting back into school.

I hear a sound, like the judge tapping his desk with a wooden hammer. I look at the judge, but his arms are folded across his chest. Hearing the sound again, and the rustling of plastic, I sit up in bed and look around.

The clock on the nightstand reads 11:55. It's pitch-black outside.

Stumbling to the window, I look out and see a sliver of light in our yard. Someone's nosing around under the tarp, shining a flashlight at the tools and supplies. It's Daryl, the neighborhood snoop. He's going through the fence posts and tools, moving the tarp to get a better look.

    I lift my blinds and the sound is enough to make him turn. He switches off his flashlight and moseys off down the road in no particular hurry.

    Daryl wasn't going to steal anything, I'm sure of that. He just has to know what's going on in everyone else's life since he doesn't have one of his own. Still, knowing he's outside our trailer at night gives me the creeps. I fall back on my bed and the dream starts up again, only stranger this time; Daryl's in it and he wants to marry my mother.

    Again, the sound of plastic and wood. I look out the window and there's Ray in the early morning light, pulling back the tarp covering the supplies. My mom goes out to give him a hug and Ray says, "Not so tight, you'll bust a rib."

    That sounds like the same old Ray, I think. But when he turns sideways and I see how thin he is, it seems like maybe he's not joking.

    Ray asks my mother to make a pot of coffee, then, seeing me in the window, says, "All right, let's get with it."

This is more like it, I think. Now that I've got him here, I don't want to lose him, so I don't mention I was going to pedal over to Alicia's ice cream parlor this afternoon. Before changing my plans, I decide to wait and see how long Ray lasts without a drink.

After a night of tossing and turning, I feel like I haven't slept at all. In the kitchen, my mom's got a pot of "motivation" brewing to keep Ray going through a long day of fence building. I've never tried coffee before but since I can barely keep my eyes open, I figure, "Why not?" I shuffle over, pour myself a cup, take a big gulp, and almost spit it out.

Kyla snorts. Laughing, Ray slides the milk and sugar across the table in my direction. "Try these," he says. I pour in a healthy dose of both and the coffee turns a creamy white and tastes a lot less bitter.

Now it's four in the afternoon and I'm exhausted from digging post holes all day.

Ray helped. He measured everything out and even started a couple of holes himself, but mostly sat on the porch drinking coffee and giving advice while I finished another hole. That, and he smoked about a million cigarettes. Once, I asked him to blow his smoke in another direction. Finally, I got mad and said, "Why don't you just quit?"

He blew out a giant cloud of smoke and said, "One habit at a time, nephew. One habit at a time." I didn't know what that meant and didn't feel like asking either.

Later, we, meaning mostly me, mixed the concrete and set sixteen posts in the sixteen holes. They're spaced out all around our back door so when my dog needs to go out, it'll be right into the yard. Tomorrow, Memorial Day, we'll install the gate and string the fencing between the posts.

While Ray goes inside to clean up, I stop and look around our yard. I'm staring at the spot I ran to on "the night in question" before my mother and the young cop showed up.

Some people think that must have been the worst night ever.

Not even close.

Because I had run to that spot before, years earlier. It was the night I grabbed Kyla and we hurried outside to escape one of my father's worst blowups. That's the night I can never seem to forget.

I was ten and my father had come home

drunker and later than usual. Waking from a sound sleep, I heard his work boots pounding on our back porch. My half-asleep brain could tell what kind of mood he was in by how much noise he made on the stairs. Loud definitely wasn't good.

My mother was asleep on the couch. Maybe she didn't jump up fast enough to ask him what kind of day he had. Maybe she didn't have his dinner waiting when he stumbled through the door. Maybe she shouldn't have married him in the first place.

Usually, he had to work himself up to a hot temper. That night, he came through the door ready to fight. He started in on her right away, saying, no wonder he didn't want to come home to "this dump of a trailer," to a woman like her, to kids like us. While she tried to reheat his dinner, he hit her the first time. Grabbing her by the arm, he spun her around and slapped her again. His plate hit the floor and he screamed at my mother to pick it up.

I was watching from the doorway, scared, but already used to the sights and sounds of his anger. My father screamed at me to "get the hell out." I stood there frozen, and then I felt Kyla standing at my elbow.

My mother pleaded with her eyes for me to take

my sister and go. That's what we talked about beforehand, but I couldn't move. When he started tossing the cups and dishes from the kitchen counter to the floor, I covered Kyla's eyes. Grabbing her hand, I pulled her toward the front door. We passed the phone on the way out, but I knew that was useless. And so was I.

I just stood there in the yard with my sister, hoping that someone would call the police. I listened and watched and prayed as my father trashed the entire trailer, and everything in it—with my mother stuck in there with him.

Maybe it wasn't the worst night ever. Maybe it just seemed that way because I was getting older and wanted to help but didn't. And I knew why. Because I was afraid.

Not because my mother told me not to help.

Not because he was twice my size.

Not because I might make things worse by trying.

Because I was afraid, and I ran to that spot in the yard and stood there, frozen, until it was all over. Later, we went to Loraine's while he slept peacefully in his own bed. No police came. No ambulance. No neighbors. Loraine brewed my mother a cup of tea and made up beds for Kyla and me, but she shouldn't have bothered with mine.

I didn't sleep a wink that night, although I usually could at Loraine's. And afterward?

I guess I seemed a little braver. I always jumped in whenever he raised a hand to my mother. But I wasn't any braver. I was more afraid than ever. Only now there was something new I was afraid of, even more than I was of him.

I was afraid to look in the mirror and see the fear in my own face.

The first few times I tried to help, my father tossed me to the side like a rag doll before starting back in on my mother. But I got bigger. I learned to time my punches. I couldn't beat him or stop him from beating me, but I could get his attention off her and onto me and that was good enough. I got taller and stronger, and I learned how to turn my fear into something I could use against him.

Sometimes, my mother would run to her room and lock the door while he was busy chasing me around. Then I'd break free and run out to the yard. And that's the way it stayed, right up until last week when it was just the two of us, me and my father, home alone. That's why I ran to that same spot. Habit.

Ever since "the night in question," I've been

acting. People expect me to be all broken up about my father dying. Okay. The same way I acted brave when I was afraid, now I act sad when I'm happy. Two things you can never admit in life: that you're afraid, or that you're happy someone died.

I hear our back door open and close. Turning, I see Ray walking down our back steps and across the yard. He steps through the spot where the new gate will be tomorrow. "Not staying for dinner?" I ask.

"I'm headin' home," he replies, and walks off down the lane. That's when I realize Ray spent the entire day here without stopping for a drink. He must have held out just to help me build my fence.

"Thanks," I shout after him, but I'm not sure he hears me. All around the yard, the fence posts are arranged like soldiers standing guard. I salute as I walk past them and back into the house.

Inside, I realize it's too late to pedal over to Alicia's, and, besides, I'm beat. I drink two glasses of water from the sink and tell my mother I'm going to take a shower. She's sitting at the kitchen table, not saying anything.

I ask about Ray, saying he didn't seem like

himself today. Although I always laugh when people say that, like who would you be if you weren't yourself? My mother tells me my uncle hasn't had a drink for three days, the longest he's gone without in fifteen years. "He's going to be all right," she says. "He just needs a little time alone right now." I'm shocked, but glad.

Maybe anything is possible.

TWENTY

I remember thinking that good things and bad things can happen in the same day, even within a few minutes of each other. Good, as in Alicia inviting me somewhere. We're standing by my locker when she asks if I'd like to come to her older brother's science fair this weekend. "Are your parents making you go?" I ask her.

"No," she laughs. "I just want to support my brother." Wow, the difference between Halvdale and Bent Oaks is a lot further than a few miles on a map. Actually, I wouldn't mind seeing a real science fair, not the third-grade version with bubbling volcanoes. But with her parents?

Alicia tells me that they've got a long van. We'll sit in the back, and then go off on our own when we get to Halvdale High. Sure, why not? All good.

Followed by bad, as in Bob Teski coming along at just that moment, slamming the locker door into my back and sprawling my books all over the hallway.

Teski and I have had some issues in the past.

Okay, Mr. Schmink says to be totally honest, so the "issue" we have is that I kicked Teski's ass in a fight at the bus stop earlier this year. I won't even say it might have been partly his fault because I'm taking full responsibility for my own actions now—another Mr. Schmink idea—so I'll just say it was all on me, one hundred percent.

Teski has been pushing for a rematch ever since. He shouts things in the hallways, tries to call me out, and I guess today he's decided to see how far he can push before I push back. Just in case, he has two of his buddies with him.

We square off and I make a fist. I'm about to swing when Alicia touches my arm and says, "Spence."

The vice principal, Mr. Sullivan, is heading straight for us.

The whole thing was a setup. Most of the guys I've fought with in the past know my situation: one more incident and I'm expelled. If we fight, they get a week's detention, but I'm out for good.

Teski knows it, and he waited until he saw Mr. Sullivan to make his move.

That doesn't exactly stop me from wanting to hit something though, and I swing my fist into the locker door and the sound echoes up and down the hallway.

Teski and his boys take off running. Alicia whispers, "Good luck," and leaves for class, and that leaves me all alone. Alone except for Mr. Sullivan, who hustles down to where I'm standing with my back turned, shouting, "What's going on here?"

My mind is spinning. I know that if I turn around all angry and shouting I'll be dragged off to the principal's office. The next stop after that is the street. Mr. Sullivan is Ms. Lepton's enforcer and not one of my biggest fans. Would he like to catch me in something like this? In a word, yes.

Then I remember something else Mr. Schmink told me: "Fake it till you make it."

Do I feel like chasing down Teski and pounding his stupid face in? Yep. And, while I'm at it, letting Mr. Sullivan know what I think of his crap-brown tie that matches his nasty yellow teeth? You bet.

Instead, I close my locker door nice and easy, turn around, and say, "Oh, hi, Mr. Sullivan. Bob Teski accidentally hit my locker door without meaning to. Knocked my books all over the place. I'll pick them up."

Then I smile, wide. I've never felt anything like that before—in the time it takes to turn around, I half calm myself down and half pretend to. I get down on the floor and start scooping up all my papers.

Talk about luck. There's a B+ from this morning's math quiz on top of the pile. Mr. Sullivan sees it. I know he does. What can he do?

He says, "All right, all right, but let's be more careful in the future, all right?"

I'm thinking, "That's a lot of 'all rights' in one sentence," but don't say it. What I do say is, "Sure, thanks," and then I check out my locker, and the only damage is a tiny dent in the door that you wouldn't even be able to see if you weren't looking for it.

Riding my bike is when I do my best thinking. Heading to the shelter, I think about what would have happened if I had thrown a punch. I'd be expelled and have to repeat eighth grade and not get a dog and lose my job and not see Alicia and watch as the judge reads a note from Ms. Lepton telling him what a low-life excuse for a human being I am, and instead . . .

Instead, I take a deep breath and see a whole movie trailer's worth of good stuff. There's me playing with my dog—tough because I don't know what he looks like yet—and me working at the shelter, and then I'm walking my dog with Alicia, and if it had gone on any longer we would have been running through a park flying a kite on a summer day or something, but that was plenty.

I picture a giant calendar as I ride. Eight days of class until graduation. Thirteen until the coroner's inquest. I tell myself, "Just keep it together." Deep breaths. In through the nose, out through the lips. I'm riding past the old cemetery when, out of nowhere, I remember another of my uncle's sayings: "Whistling past the graveyard."

TWENTY-ONE

For most boys Caleb's age, the upcoming summer vacation means sleeping late and swimming at the local pond. For Caleb, it means extra work. His father pushes him day and night to finish his farm chores, and afterward to help train the dogs. Sleeping late is not an option.

Despite the loss of Spike, the previous weekend's fights had been a success. Mr. Lime returned from Chicago with a thousand dollars in profit and a smile on his face. The smile wouldn't last long. Caleb could testify to that. Now, with more fights scheduled at home the following weekend, there's work to be done.

Caleb's job this morning is to "chain out" the next batch of fighters. Each of the dogs is taken to a spot in the yard where they're chained to a tractor tire or other heavy weight. Mr. Lime likes to keep his dogs unsocialized. Separating them from other people, and each other, keeps the animals more in his control. The dogs are freed only for exercise sessions, tune-up fights, or trips to the shed where they're injected with steroids or antibiotics.

Lime instructs his son to give the dogs just enough food, shade, and water to keep them healthy. But he is to make their lives miserable enough that they are at their "nastiest" when Lime brings them into the pit for their next fight.

Caleb nods and follows his father's orders, his face never betraying his true feelings. Inside, he smiles at the secret he's been carrying around all week.

The previous weekend, with his father away in Chicago, Caleb had hitched a ride into River City and walked around town. Sitting on the courthouse steps, he felt like an escaped prisoner. How long had it been since he'd gone anywhere without his father knowing his whereabouts?

If this feeling of freedom was exciting, it was about to get better. Out of nowhere, after years of wondering where she might be, his mother had reached out to him. Knowing how dangerous her ex-husband was, she had gotten an old friend to approach Caleb in town. Whispering, "God bless you," the friend pressed a note into his hand.

Before unfolding the sheet of lined paper, Caleb glanced nervously around the village square. The note explained how sorry his mother was for leaving him years before and invited him to meet with her "out West, if you want to."

Here was the truth of the night she'd fled—not the version Caleb had heard so often from his father. His mother explained how, after yet another beating, she had run away with only the clothes on her back and without her son. Her husband had threatened to kill her if she returned for Caleb, and she believed him.

Calling the authorities for help, she was warned by Sheriff Robertson, "Don't come back here under any circumstances."

Eight years later, still fearful of Lime, her note tells her son to "leave a message after you arrive in Denver, and wait for me to call back." It took Caleb roughly one minute to forgive his mother, and one more to begin planning his escape.

Caleb could only imagine what his mother had gone through married to a man like Lime. Not much older than Caleb was now, she'd done the best she could by running as far away as possible. Now he would join her, and they would begin a new life together. Why wait until his eighteenth birthday, when he could be gone in a matter of weeks? Maybe right after the next dogfight?

With no money of his own, Caleb plans to finance his trip by "borrowing" his father's cash. On fight nights, the stack of bills in Lime's safe sometimes tops five thousand dollars.

A pretty good start to a new life, Caleb thinks.

He decides that since he's borrowing his father's money, he'll borrow his pickup truck, as well. Caleb doesn't have a license, but he can drive. Next Saturday night, after a full work week and a night of dogfights, his father will sleep like a baby.

By the time he wakes late Sunday morning, his son, cash, and truck will be hundreds of miles away.

Caleb laughs, wondering what his father will miss most: his money, his truck, or his son. He knows how his father feels about money, but he also really loves that pickup. His son, he's sure, will come in a distant third in that contest. Caleb's only regret is that he won't be around to see the look on the old man's face when he discovers his loss.

His father always refers to a dog with a sad look as a "punk." Maybe, by next Sunday afternoon, with no truck, no cash, and no helper to do all the heavy work around the farm, Jeremiah Lime will wear that same look. Punk.

TWENTY-TWO

I'm liking Blue more every day. One look at his scars tells me he shouldn't trust people, or other dogs, but he's starting to.

I'm liking Josie more lately, too. I know she's heard about my father by now. She lives like a hermit out here with her dogs and other animals, but she still has her friends in town: other volunteers, adopters, neighbors. I'm sure someone's told her the gossip about my family, but she hasn't said a word.

Maybe she's waiting for me to talk about it. Maybe when everything settles down, I will.

Back home after work, I stop and admire our new fence. There it is all finished with the fencing strung between the posts and a gate that I swing open to pull my bike through. Pulling it closed, I listen as it clicks shut behind me.

It sounds as good as it looks.

I plan on walking my dog, when I get one, most of the time, but it's nice to have a fenced yard for the times when I can't. Or, when I just want to let him outside to run around and act like a dog.

In the kitchen, Ray's sitting at the table, watching while my mother teaches Kyla a recipe. This is new. Up until now, my sister's treated the kitchen as a place to drop her books on the table, and to look in the fridge to see what my mother's brought home from the diner.

"I'm going to be a professional chef," Kyla announces.

"Great!" I say. "And great to hear you talking," I think, but don't say out loud.

Ray looks about a thousand percent better than yesterday. I notice he's drinking water, nothing stronger. Apparently, he worked his half day at the foundry, then spent the afternoon finishing the gate—which we didn't get to yesterday.

When I thank him, he just laughs and says, "It was done when I got here."

My mother tells me Kyla's making pot roast for dinner and that I'm setting the table and doing the dishes. "So wash up. It's almost ready."

The meal's good and I have seconds of everything. I think to myself that maybe, just maybe, my family's starting to see how things can be around here without my father. But I don't want to jinx it, so I don't say anything. I'm putting the last of the dishes in the sink when I notice something, or someone, loitering on our back porch. It's Daryl.

Daryl's one of those neighborhood guys who you're never really sure how you got to know him in the first place.

I guess he was a friend of my father's, meaning they would talk out by the road sometimes if Daryl happened to be walking by—and Daryl seemed to be walking by an awful lot.

Some friend. My father's been gone less than two weeks and Daryl keeps coming around trying to cozy up to my mother. Now it looks like he's tired of waiting by the road, so he's hanging around our back door, which is where I see him now.

Most people knock when they reach your door; Daryl just stands there. "Ahem," I say, and gesture toward the figure on our back porch.

Because she's nice to everyone, my mother says, "Well, I guess we should invite him in." Hearing this, Kyla gets up from the table and stomps down the hall to her room, slamming the door behind her.

My sister's not as nice as my mother, I guess.

Daryl stumbles into our kitchen, acting all surprised, like he wasn't just lurking around, waiting to be asked inside. Ray gives him a nod, and I just keep washing dishes, making as much noise as possible.

My mom offers Daryl a cup of coffee. "Uh-oh," I think. "Now you'll never get rid of him." Daryl's thing, now that my father's gone, is to offer to help us out around our trailer, even though we never asked for any help, or want it, especially from him. Sometimes, my mother is just too damned nice.

I turn around and notice Ray's looking pretty tired. He was probably about to head home when Daryl showed up. If Daryl's a chess game, I'm already two moves ahead of my mother. I watch her and wait, and there it is. She knows she's made the wrong move.

Kyla's locked in her room, I'm about to head to mine, and Ray's halfway out of his seat. She'll be stuck here with Daryl when we go.

Even my mother's not that nice. She pours Ray some more coffee, brings over fresh milk and sugar, puts her hand on his shoulder, and practically shoves him back down in his seat. "So, how have you been, Daryl?" she asks.

Seeing Daryl sitting in my father's chair seems wrong. It gets me comparing the two of them. Daryl's the same age that my father was and even looks a little bit like him. Except that my father was more athletic, and Daryl is, well, Daryl.

For my father, sports were important, and the best time of his life was high school, especially freshman and sophomore years. After that, my grandfather made him quit sports to work in his shop after school every day. But for those first two years, he played on every team he could, sometimes even two in the same season, like wrestling and basketball. That was easy back then because Halvdale never had enough players trying out for anything except football.

My father made varsity in three sports as a sophomore, and the next year, he had to tell his coaches that he couldn't play anymore.

It's stuff like that that made me feel sorry for him sometimes, even though he turned into such a jerk later.

But who knows. What if he had kept playing? Maybe he'd have gotten a scholarship, gotten out of this neighborhood, not started drinking, and then who knows how his life might have ended up?

Mr. Schmink is always reminding me to forget about all the who-knows and what-ifs in my essays. The point is to deal with things the way they are, and not get all daydreamy about what could have been. According to Mr. Schmink, anyway.

    For Daryl, the best time of his life was in the army. I know because he never shuts up about it. He served three tours. He calls them "tours," but mostly he was in Fort Hood and didn't do much touring from what I can tell. He didn't do any fighting, and he never got a promotion past private. Mostly, he just worked on jeeps.

    And even though he loved the army, he didn't make it like a career or anything, so try to figure that one out. The only part he never talks about is why he left, so maybe he got fired or something.

    Can you even get fired from the army? My father told me once that he thought Daryl was a DD, meaning dishonorable discharge. If that's true, I guess it's why he never talks about it.

    Mostly, I think Daryl was one of those soldiers who was good at keeping his gear all clean and stowed away perfectly. That's what he calls his stuff, his gear. I bet his boots shined like a mirror. Also, I think he was really good at taking orders. Like "Yes, Sergeant," and "Yes, Lieutenant," but if he had to come up with any ideas of his own, he'd be in serious trouble. He probably needed some four-star general to wake him up in the morning and another one to tell him to go to bed at night.

Now Daryl works at the Chevy dealership in town, and he talks about it the same way he talks about the army. These days, instead of saving the rest of the world, he's saving Halvdale.

But the thing that absolutely drives me crazy about Daryl is the way he pesters my sister.

Kyla doesn't like talking to people lately, especially people she doesn't like, but Daryl can't take the hint. He asks her all these questions. "Kyla, are you studying algebraic expressions yet?" "Kyla, have you learned about the Constitution yet?" Or, even, "Kyla, do you have a boyfriend?"

Then he stares, waiting for an answer. My mom usually answers for her, or Kyla will mumble her way through it, but you can tell it bothers her. If it bothers her a little, it bothers me a lot.

Sometimes, I feel like going to the shelf for our old encyclopedia, dropping it in Daryl's lap, and saying, "Here, you want to know about the Constitution? Look it up, Private."

Without even meaning to, my uncle saves the day. He's so tired, he's falling asleep in his chair. My mother notices and offers to drive him home. She calls down the hall to Kyla, grabs her car keys, and herds us all toward the front door.

Daryl looks at his half-finished coffee like this is the diner and he might ask for a to-go cup. Then he sees the look on my mother's face and decides that's probably not a wise idea.

After locking the door behind us, my mother tells Daryl it was nice to see him before firing up the station wagon and turning on the car lights. As we pull away, I look back at Daryl, standing all alone in the road and looking sad.

After dropping off Ray, we get back home and Kyla heads for the TV. My mother yells, "No TV. Homework." Kyla turns obediently for her bedroom. I'm on my way to mine when my mother stops me in the hallway. "You know, I talked to a lawyer once," she says, surprising me.

"What? When?" I ask.

"Before, about a year ago. And I went to the police station and talked to a detective about getting away from him." *Him.* She doesn't say "my husband" or "your father," but I know who she means. "They wouldn't help. Nobody would help. I was afraid if he found out, he'd kill me, but I never gave up." She gives me a hug and doesn't seem to want to let go.

"I'm sorry," I say.

"Me too," she says before turning for her room and closing the door behind her.

TWENTY-THREE

I promised not to get into another fight on school property. So far, so good. I just have to stay off the bus and on my bike. Today, I'm pedaling away from the junior high when Teski pops out the front door. He's yelling a lot of stupid stuff, and loud enough for everyone to hear.

Personal stuff about my father and my sister, and just to make sure he's got my attention, my mother.

Okay, he wants my attention and he's got it.

I point to the street leading to the Quik-Mart and turn my bike around. A lot of people hang out there after school, drinking slushies and smoking cigarettes, so he knows where I'm headed.

I get there first, pull around the back, and wait.

Teski has a two-block walk to think things over. Maybe he'll change his mind, maybe he won't. I noticed his two buddies were with him, but that doesn't worry me. They're more like cheerleaders than fighters. If Teski goes down quick, like I hope he will, his pals aren't going to do anything.

I'm calm as I walk to the area between the dumpster and the store. I look up in the clouds for Skylab, this space station that's supposed to come crashing back to earth any day now. We talked about it in class today. No one is sure where or when it will hit, but you might see it burning up as it reenters the atmosphere. You might even find a piece in your own backyard.

I smile, thinking about our new fence. Whatever falls inside the yard belongs to us. We won't have to share Skylab with the neighbors.

Sometimes, I think being this calm should worry me. Everything slows down for me right before a fight. I can see everything more clearly, and it's like I know what's going to happen before it does. Even my heart rate slows down, I swear.

I always laughed at my father's cop shows and the criminals who got all nervous before they committed a crime. Later, when some cop asked them what happened, they'd blurt out, "It all happened so fast, it was like a blur."

That's when you knew they were lying. I mean, if you're a criminal and you're out doing criminal things every day, why get nervous? It's your job, right? That would be like the milkman saying he gets nervous every time he delivers a quart of low-fat.

Long before I see Teski, I hear him. When I look around, here he comes, followed by his two goons.

He looks as nervous as one of the TV criminals, but tries to hide it by acting tough. His buddies shout encouragement—from a distance. Looking around to see if he's got an audience, Teski starts trash-talking. Curious about all the noise, people are drifting back from the front of the store.

The whole thing reminds me of the Oaks, when the locals sense a fight coming. A lot of spectators who don't mind seeing a fight, as long as they're not the ones getting hit.

Teski's pals stand behind him, thinking the best place to be is covering their loud-mouthed buddy's back: that's exactly where I want them.

I'm feeling confident. We're way off school property, and hidden from the street. The local cops roll by here occasionally to keep an eye on things, but I plan to be on my bike and halfway to Josie's before anyone "official" arrives on the scene. It's time to start. I haven't said a word. Teski keeps yammering away until I ask, "Are you going to fight, or talk?"

I can't believe it. He talks more now than before. He won't shut up, and he won't fight. He wants to put on a show.

I remember the night the young cop came to our trailer and challenged my old man. I walk up close to Teski with my hands at my sides and say, "You want to take a shot at me?"

He keeps talking. His friends are laughing. Everyone else is wondering if it's a fight or a prank. I'm starting to wonder myself. He's mentioned my dead father, my mother, my sister, and I'm thinking even Mr. Schmink would understand if I took a swing.

The next thing I hear is, "How's Alicia? Tell her I'm going to—" *Whack.* I was going to use a straight left hand followed by a right hook, but Teski makes it easy. He's talking when he should be listening.

I catch him flush with the first punch, so I repeat it. Three more lefts to the face, and he crumples to the pavement. He's mumbling, still trying to form words. One buddy props him up, while the other tries to revive him with sips of neon-blue slushie.

"You too?" I say. Neither one answers. It's over.

The only thing I feel on the way to the shelter is tired. I think it's from all the bike riding I've been doing lately, but maybe not. It's the same way I always feel after a fight, just like I'm calm beforehand. I don't know what that means.

By tomorrow, everyone at school will know what happened. Ms. Lepton? I hope not. Alicia? I better tell her before she hears it from someone else. That means pedaling over to Josie's, working three hours, back to Alicia's house in Halvdale, and then home for a late dinner and homework before hitting the sack around eleven.

Tomorrow morning, I have to be up early to bike to school. Do the people on my old bus wonder why I'm pedaling down the side of the road as they pass me each morning? I see Miller through the bus window every day but haven't talked to him in a while. Maybe I'll stop by his trailer this weekend, just like the old days. Or he can come over to my place. My father's not around to say he can't.

I see the shelter up ahead and pull into the driveway. Inside, I see Blue. He sees me too, and his tail starts to wag.

TWENTY-FOUR

We're in Alicia's van, driving to the science fair. Her parents are up front, and her little brother, Bobby, is in the center seat, fast asleep. Her parents shout a couple of questions to me in the back. Nothing too personal, mostly about classes that Alicia and I have together, and, for most of the ride, we all sit there with phony smiles plastered to our faces.

Alicia's older brother, Tim, is already at the fair. He got up at six a.m. to catch a ride to an event that doesn't begin until nine.

Mentally, I scratch science fairs off the list of activities I want to try. I'm thinking something that starts a little later in the day might be a better choice.

I watch Alicia's father in the rearview, and wonder if he's heard about my father. Definitely not, I decide, or I wouldn't be here with his daughter. I remind myself not to let anything slip about the Oaks or my family, and I keep my mouth shut for most of the ride.

As promised, after arriving at Halvdale High, Alicia and I head off to explore the place. She waves to her parents and brother as they wander off in the opposite direction.

Today's a first for me. I've never gone to a school function that wasn't required before—classes, detention. It's hard to believe, but a few months from now, if I'm not taking classes at some other state institution, this is where I'll be going to school.

As far as the science fair goes, I'm kind of liking it. The projects are by freshmen and sophomores and make up half of their final grade in chemistry, biology, physics, whatever. I laugh when I see Alicia's brother's project, an erupting volcano. But his is activated by a computer keyboard. Punching in the right code sends a message that starts an electronic explosion and light show that he can do over and over.

Alicia and I hang around and watch experiments and sit in the bleachers along with other brothers, sisters, parents, and grandparents. We eat hot dogs and pretzels from the cafeteria, walk the empty hallways, and wait for the voting on best projects—a long day.

I recognize a couple of kids from school, and even one from Bent Oaks. Luckily, he doesn't see me, or maybe he does, and he's doing the same thing I'm doing, which is avoiding anyone else from Bent Oaks.

Also, we kiss for the first time in one of those hallways—not the kid from Bent Oaks—Alicia and I. It's all nice and natural, and I'm not sure if I started it or she did, but the best part is that it's out of the way. Don't get me wrong, it was very enjoyable, but now there won't be any more stress about that "first kiss." Like, "Is now a good time?" or "Should I wait until we get back tonight?"

Later, just to make sure there's no tension about the second kiss, we do it again.

Something else happens in that hallway—I see a picture of my father. Two, actually. Outside the gym is a huge trophy case, and there he is with his teammates, lined up next to a bus before a road trip. Halvdale's one and only state title game.

My father wasn't the star player—he was still only a sophomore. But he might have been, if my grandfather hadn't made him quit sports. It gets to me sometimes, thinking about all the might-have-beens.

I'm amazed at how much he looks like me, or I look like him, I guess. He even looks happy, smiling with his teammates. I go into one of my zones and the next thing I know, Alicia's looking at the side of my face, asking, "Spence, are you okay?"

"My father," I say, pointing to the pictures. For a few seconds, she looks as surprised as me, then she turns and walks away. Catching up, I ask her, "Hey, what's up?"

"Yeah, it's just . . ." She walks a few steps farther, and stops.

"What?" I ask.

She says, "It's hard, you know . . ." She picks her words carefully. "I mean, as much as everyone probably wants you to talk about it, it's hard not talking about it, too."

That's when I realize we've never said a word about my father, or my suspension, or why I was gone, and why I'm back. It's funny, with most people, I don't want to talk about "the night in question." But here's someone who tried to help me by waiting for me to bring it up. And I never did.

Suddenly, I find myself telling her everything: Bent Oaks, my father, the beatings, the police, my sister and mother, all of it. Maybe I should practice talking more often because once I get started I can't stop. I tell Alicia that I know she's heard things, like where I'm from and that my father died drunk and that I was alone with him that night.

"But that's all people know. The rest they get from their imagination. And soon, maybe, it will all be over."

When I finally shut up, Alicia looks at me a long time. I can't tell if she's angry, sad, or just surprised at everything I just told her. Finally, she tells me she doesn't listen to other people's version of things anyway. I must have covered just about everything because when I ask if she has any questions, she says no. She just gives me a hug and a smile.

Turning to leave, I notice a guy around my father's age standing at the trophy case. He's with a woman, his wife probably, and they're pointing at some of the same pictures Alicia and I were looking at.

Was he one of my father's teammates?

If I asked about John MacElliott, class of 1961, would he remember the smiling kid I saw in those pictures?

Alicia and I work our way back down the hallway to the gym. The votes will be coming in soon and the day is winding down. But I can't help looking back at the trophy case, and the possible one-time friend of a young, happy John MacElliott.

After the fair, we pile back into Alicia's van, this time with her older brother, Tim, in the middle seat next to their little brother, Bobby. Tim turns around and asks his sister, "So, how'd you like my project?"

"It was okay," she replies.

Tim laughs, then asks my name for the second time. He hardly seems upset that his project lost by one vote to the dork with the solar-powered hat. "Can't win 'em all," he says. Halfway out of the parking lot, Alicia's parents offer to drive me home, but I say no thank you.

I planned ahead. My bike is hidden in some bushes around the corner from Alicia's house so that no one can drive me back to Bent Oaks.

TWENTY-FIVE

After a week of school and work and pedaling all over town, I sleep about twelve hours Saturday night, which makes me late for work Sunday morning.

I call Josie, saying I'm on my way and run outside to hop on my bike. That's when Daryl, who "just happens" to be driving by, offers me a ride. I try to figure how many ways this could go wrong, but, mostly, I'm really late, so I throw my bike in his trunk and say, "Sure, thanks."

On the ride over, Daryl keeps dropping hints about how much he likes my mom, and how he wants to "take things to the next level."

When we get to the shelter, I can see that he wants to come inside, but that's the last thing I want. After five minutes, he'd be lecturing Josie on how to raise the dogs and run her business.

Then I think, that might be interesting, watching as Josie grabs her shotgun while Pal and a dozen other dogs dismantle Daryl. This seems like one of those times to do the adult thing and lie, so I say, "There's some kennel cough going around, and we're keeping people out for a while, but thanks for the ride."

The funny thing about lying is that it usually works, if you don't do it too often.

I try not to do it at all, but there are times when you know the world expects you to lie. Maybe even at the coroner's inquest, but I'm not totally sure about that one yet. I've pretty much decided that I won't lie unless someone on the other side lies about me first. Then, like Ray says, "All bets are off."

Lying to Daryl seems pretty easy though, maybe too easy, since he's not the sharpest tool in the shed. I guess that's where you have to be careful. Not everyone is as dumb as Daryl.

Weekends at the shelter are for "special projects." Today's is a water leak in the dog run. We've got the water turned off and the dogs in their pens while we figure out how to fix it. Otherwise, the dogs will be living in a swimming pool. Josie puts together a list of plumbing supplies and leaves me in charge while she drives over to the hardware store.

"In charge" sounds pretty good. Mostly, though, I'm just hoping the phone doesn't ring and nobody shows up before she gets back.

While I mop up, I'm thinking about yesterday and Alicia's 2-2-2 family. That's her description: two kids, two dogs, two cars. "The American dream," she said, laughing.

"But there's three kids in your house," I told her.

"Yeah," she said. "I think someone left my little brother in a basket on the front porch one night."

The whole driving to the science fair, hanging with the neighbors, and eating hot dogs thing was just another weekend to them, but to me it was like something out of a movie. I mean, I know how to act around drunk people or sitting-on-the-porch-complaining-about-life people or standing-in-the-road-screaming-at-the-kids people, but normal people? Not so much.

Some of our neighbors in the Oaks say they hate the people in Halvdale. They say they hate them because they hate us, which sounds kind of shaky to me. I don't think most people in Halvdale really spend all that much time thinking about us. They're too busy painting their houses, cutting their lawns, and driving to science fairs.

Mr. Schmink lives in Halvdale and he's all right. Alicia's family was okay, and I know kids at school from there and they seem all right, too.

I'm starting to think if my mom wants to escape the Oaks like when she was young, maybe we can just move to Halvdale. That way I could stay in the same school district but not have to live in Bent Oaks.

I'm thinking all of this while I work, daydreaming, as usual, when the ringing of the phone snaps me out of it. Inside, I pick up and listen as a kid around my age—he sounds like my age—asks about dogs for adoption. I tell him you have to be eighteen to adopt a dog. He says that's fine. The dog is for his father.

The kid says the dog they're looking for belonged to his father once before. He goes on to tell me that the dog escaped from their yard in Chicago, or maybe it was stolen by dogfighters, he's not sure. He tells me he's calling all the shelters in the state, and then he describes his dog. A pit bull, about forty-five pounds, black coat, so black he's almost deep blue, with white on his chest and paws. Maybe he's scarred from being in dogfights. Have I seen any dogs like that?

That sounds a lot like Blue.

I know the guy who brought him here on his day off was from Chicago, so that fits. I ask the kid when his dog was lost, and he says about two weeks ago, and that fits, too. I tell him about Blue and that he might be the one they're looking for, but no way to tell without stopping by.

I give him our address. He's already got our phone number, and he says maybe he and his father will visit us soon.

After he hangs up I feel that tingle I always get when something bad is about to happen. Something seems odd about the call. I'm still thinking about it when Josie pulls back into the driveway.

We get to work on the water pipe. I loosen the joint above the leak, Josie cuts it with a hacksaw, and when we fit it together with the piece from the hardware store, not a drop leaks out. I wish Ray was here to see my handiwork. Afterward, it's back to the usual walking, cleaning, and feeding, along with a couple of visits from people looking to adopt dogs.

I don't remember the phone call until I'm walking Blue at the end of the day. When I tell Josie about it, she stops and listens, then has me repeat every detail of the conversation.

"Something's not right," she says. "Dogfighters use all kinds of tricks to get dogs from shelters, sometimes to fight, sometimes as 'bait' dogs. This one's more specific though. He's looking for a particular dog that he lost."

"What do we know about Blue?" she asks me.

"Well, he's been in some fights, that's for sure."

"Right, and how did he get here?"

"Brought in by a guy from Chicago," I say.

"Right, again. Now we've got another guy who misses his dog so much that he calls every shelter in the state to find him, but . . ."

"But he waits two weeks to do it," I add.

"And he somehow just knows dogfighters took him and he 'might' have some scars," Josie adds. "I looked Blue over when he arrived here," she says. "I'd bet my life that some of those scars are two years old."

"I'm sorry," I say. "I didn't know."

"How could you? Okay, not a problem. If they show up, they can't take him without proof that he's theirs. I doubt that they have any proof. And if they call again, I'll talk to them."

While I'm finishing my chores, I think about the voice on the phone. He didn't sound like a dogfighter, but what does a dogfighter sound like? Not a kid, I guess.

I'm mad at myself for giving this stranger so much information.

I screwed up and I know it.

I think about how much better Blue's been doing lately. I've been walking him with Pal, and we've been letting him out in the run with the other dogs—no problems. He's pretty chill at feeding times, too.

If I were Blue, and I went through what I think he went through, I don't think I'd be so forgiving. Dogs are amazing that way. Even if no one adopts him, Josie said he could live here forever. I'd help pay for his keep if it comes to that. I make a vow to work as many hours as I can so I can be here when the kid and his father show up.

Mr. Schmink always says, "Every problem has a solution." He's right. I fixed the problem with my father and I'll fix this one too.

TWENTY-SIX

Ordering Caleb to tag along, Jeremiah Lime unlocks his gate, and father and son begin the four-hour drive to Halvdale, Illinois.

Caleb closes his eyes for most of the trip. He's seen enough of the Midwest for a lifetime. Reading a comic book, he dreams of the day when he can leave Indiana, and his father, in his rearview mirror forever. As usual, Lime Sr. barely seems to notice his son sitting beside him. He squeezes the steering wheel in anticipation of being reunited with a prized fighting dog.

Approaching Halvdale, Lime cautions his son to say nothing upon their arrival at Pal's Place and to let him do the talking. But he's wasting his breath. Caleb usually says nothing and always lets his father do the talking.

Seeing the sign for the animal shelter up ahead, Lime instructs his son, "We're here to adopt a family pet. If they ask any more than that, tell 'em it's to replace your dog who died."

Caleb thinks, "That's actually true," and remembers a little black-and-white terrier from his past. Lucky wasn't much of a fighter, but Caleb had grown to love the playful pit bull. His father, however, had no patience for "useless dogs that didn't pull their weight."

Caleb had asked his father for more time to work with the young dog, but Lime grew more and more irritated with the pup. One day, angered by his refusal to fight, Lime took Lucky behind the barn and Caleb heard the echo of a single pistol shot.

After burying Lucky's remains in the pit behind the kennel, Caleb willed himself to never again care for another dog—or person. If you didn't care, maybe it wouldn't hurt so much when they died. Or when they left, like his mother had when he was seven.

Before Lucky, Caleb and his father occasionally had dogs as house pets that were never involved in fighting. Caleb vaguely remembers another pup, Whistle, who used to follow his mother around the house. Whistle had been treated like a member of the family, although Caleb couldn't remember seeing him after his mother had left.

Had his mother taken the dog with her? Not likely if she had to run away with only the clothes on her back and leave her son behind.

If Whistle disappeared around the time his mother left, there was a good chance his remains were also in the pit.

Caleb thinks of all the people who visit animal shelters looking for their lost dogs. How some of them are lucky enough to be reunited with their pets and thank the shelter owner about a million times before bringing their four-legged friend back home.

As his father pulls their pickup into the drive, Caleb looks around at Pal's Place. He hopes that Spike isn't here—that somehow he got free from the house in Chicago and is living with a loving family, far away from his father and dogfighting. If he is here, Caleb knows that his father will do anything he can, legal or otherwise, to bring him back to the farm.

As they park in the drive behind Josie's shelter, Caleb notices his father shaking with excitement. A fighting dog means more to Lime than any human being Caleb can think of, including him. He stays in the truck and watches as his father ignores the front door and works his way to the brick building out back.

TWENTY-SEVEN

The dogs are making their usual racket, so I don't notice the man stepping through the side door into the kennel. I figure Josie must be on the phone and sent him out. "Hi," I say. "Can I help you?"

"Maybe," the man booms. "I'm looking for a dog."

"We've got plenty of dogs," I tell him.

I don't mind taking a break, and I've shown a few people around before, so I know the routine. I point out some of our new arrivals and ask the usual questions: What kind of dog is he interested in? Any other dogs in the house? Puppy or old-timer? House or apartment? Basically, I've got Josie's spiel memorized and I recite it as best I can.

The guy asks almost as many questions as I do: What's my name? Do I live around here? He likes the sound of his own voice. We take a walk up one row of cages and down the other, and when we get to Blue's cage, the man goes silent.

Stopping midstride, he stares at Blue, who hangs his head and drops to the floor. This is not the same Blue we've been seeing around the kennel for the past couple of weeks. Lately, he's been a model citizen. If he weren't covered with muscles and scars you'd think he was some kid's lost puppy dog. He skulks to the back of his cage.

So excited he practically shouts, the man says, "That's the one!"

That's exactly what I'm thinking. That's the one all right, the one whose son I talked to on the phone the other day. The way Blue is acting tells me this guy is his previous owner, and that everything his son told me was a pack of lies. Okay, maybe Blue was their dog, but he was no family pet.

I take a closer look at the man. He's average height, stocky, big shoulders and hands, with a loud voice, and likes to talk like he's the boss of everything. I'm feeling that same electric tingle I used to get with my father. I stand still and watch and wait.

Where the heck is Josie? is all I can think. When the guy starts to open Blue's cage, I put myself in between him and the latch.

"Wait a second," I say. "He might run off. Let me get a leash." I move into Blue's cage and lead him back toward the open door. He doesn't want to come out, so I ask the man to step aside and give him some room. So far, this person knows my name and that I live in Bent Oaks, which he small-talked out of me. He doesn't know that I talked to Josie about his son's phone call. I wish I knew more about him.

"I'll take him," the man says, like it's a done deal.

"There's paperwork," I say, still holding Blue's leash as we make our way across the yard toward the house.

I see a gray pickup parked in the driveway with a "Farm USA" sticker peeling off its rear bumper. Swinging closer to the truck, I can just make out a passenger. It's a kid, maybe fifteen, listening to the radio. If I didn't know it before, I do now. These are the dogfighters who called about Blue.

While I'm looking at the truck, the guy grabs Blue's leash from my hand. Now he's got Blue and I'm afraid he'll bolt for his truck and leave me standing in the driveway. "There's a twenty-dollar fee," I say as calm as I can. "And that paperwork."

What's he thinking? Hard to tell, but I'm hoping it's something like, "Why steal the dog when I can pay a lousy twenty dollars and be on my way, all nice and legal." The guy shoots me a cold grin, hesitates for a moment, then turns and follows me through the open back door. Blue strains at the leash as the man pulls him inside.

Josie's at the front door, studying the pickup parked in her drive. I can see she's trying to make sense of what's happening: a truck without a driver, a passenger waiting in her driveway, and now this man pulling Blue on a leash. He must have parked around back, then worked his way to the kennel without stopping at the office.

Still, she greets him politely. "Hello," she says.

The man spits his sentences, like he's in a big hurry and we're slowing him down. "I'll take this dog," he says.

Trying to sound all "business as usual," I tell Josie that this is the man whose son called about Blue the other day. "He wants to adopt him."

"His name's Spike," the man corrects me. "He ran away from home. We've been looking all over."

"We call him Blue," Josie replies, keeping her cool. "Tell me, where did he run away from?"

"Up in Chicago," the man answers. If he's got any more of an explanation, he's not giving it. He acts like he owns the place, even though he's never set foot in the shelter before. Josie tells him there are forms to fill out and a waiting period. He pretends not to hear any of it. While she rummages through her desk, there's a knock at the front door. "Get that, will you, Spence," she asks.

I open the door and the kid, maybe a year or two older, but not any bigger than me, says, "I'm looking for my father."

"Great," I think, now there are two of them to deal with.

Pal sits on the couch, staring first at the man and then the boy. He lets out a low growl. Blue pulls as far away as he can get from this strange man, who I think is no stranger to him, and hugs the floor. He's scared, even more than the first time I saw him looking out at me from his darkened cage.

Crossing the room with the adoption papers in her hand, Josie asks innocently, "Are you sure Blue is the same dog that ran away in Chicago?"

"I should know my own dog, and the name's Spike," he replies.

Josie is probably three inches taller than the stranger. Looking down at him calmly, she says, "Because your truck has Indiana plates, so I was curious."

The electricity in the air is buzzing like a live wire. I'm not sure exactly what's happening, but I know it's not good. Standing next to the man's son, I can feel him tense up, probably not for the first time with a father like this.

The man breathes in and out a couple of times, then pretends to be reasonable. "I do business in Chicago and live in Indiana," he says.

Josie hands him the adoption papers and returns to the kitchen, putting some distance between herself and the two visitors. Once there, she says, "After you fill those out and leave a twenty-dollar deposit, there's a three-day waiting period to adopt."

The man explodes when he hears this. He's done being reasonable, or even pretending. "I'm not adopting a dog. I'm claiming my lost dog that ended up in your shelter!" His son gives him a look and the man calms himself, a little.

Turning slowly toward Josie, he forces a smile and says, "Tell you what, lady, I'll give you a reward. Sort of a finder's fee for taking care of my dog." He reaches for his wallet and pulls out a hundred-dollar bill. I notice because I've never seen one before. He waves the money in Josie's direction.

Not budging from the kitchen, Josie calls back, "If he's your dog, maybe you know where he got all those scars?"

"I don't know." The man shrugs. "He must have gotten them on the street."

"Some of those scars are two years old," she challenges him. "He didn't get them in the last two weeks."

The man's tired of talking. Turning, he pushes his son toward the front door. "I deal with dogs every day," she calls after him, "and I know what you used Blue for—dogfighting." The man doesn't reply and Josie's words hang in the air.

Finally, the man takes a slow turn, puffs his chest out, and says, "Lady, I'll use my dog for anything I damn well please. And no woman, or kid, is gonna stop me." He takes a breath. "Now, I'm being as reasonable as I can. You can take the hundred, or not, but we're on our way."

When the man moves again, so do I, blocking his path. He bumps me with his chest, once, twice, backing me closer to the front door. "Blue's already spoken for," I say.

"By who?" he demands as he tries to step around me. Pal's growling louder now and Blue's nails scratch the floor as he's dragged toward the door.

"By me," I say, holding my ground. "I filled out the application this morning. And I put in my twenty-dollar application fee, too, so I guess you're too late." I look around, feeling a punch coming, but not knowing if it will be from the man or his son, who's standing behind me and to my right.

"He's right," Josie calls from across the room.

The man lets out a big laugh. "I guess it just slipped your mind, eh, lady?"

"I'm afraid it did," Josie says.

The man calls to his son. "Open the door, Caleb." He has Blue's leash in one hand and I'm waiting for the punch that's headed my way from the other. He surprises me by reaching out and sliding the folded hundred into my shirt pocket. "Nice try, kid," he says as he yanks hard on the leash connected to Blue, who lets out a whimper.

In the kitchen, Josie lifts the shotgun from its rack. I see her and step back and away from the man, flattening myself against the living room wall. "Don't," she says. Her thumb is resting on the gun's twin hammers. She's not pointing the gun directly at the strangers, but more or less in their general direction. I don't know a lot about shotguns, but I'm thinking general direction is probably close enough.

The man turns to face Josie and the twin barrels. "You use that scatter gun to keep the dogs in line?" he asks coldly.

"It's not for the dogs," she says.

The shotgun in Josie's hands, the surprise on the man's face, Pal growling at the stranger, his son looking on almost bored. The whole thing reminds me of one of my father's cop shows. I don't recognize the next voice I hear, until I realize it's mine. "I'll take him," I say. Mindful of the shotgun, I step around the man and ease Blue's leash from his hand.

The man's son speaks next, almost in a whisper: "C'mon, Dad, let's get out of here. Come on." He stares at me as he takes his father by the arm and pulls him toward the open door.

The man won't give up. On the porch, he reaches into his wallet and produces another bill. "Lady, I'll give you two hundred dollars for that dog, right now, cash money."

"He's not for sale," Josie says flatly.

"How about you, Spencer? He's supposed to be your dog, isn't he?"

"He's not for sale," I hear myself repeating.

"Tell you what, you can keep the hundred in your pocket and here's two more. That's three hundred dollars for a broken-down fighting dog." I think about crossing to the door and slamming it shut but can't stop staring at the shotgun. I grip Blue's leash and say nothing. "Suit yourself," the man says as his son pulls him away from the house, back toward their pickup.

"Maybe we'll see you again sometime!" he shouts from the driveway. "Maybe real soon!" He's still shouting as his son opens the driver's door and pushes him inside.

Walking Blue back to the kitchen, I let out a long breath and ask, "What was that all about?"

"Get his plate number," Josie snaps, and I race to the window for a look. I call out the truck's license number while Josie scribbles it on a pad at her desk.

"You saw how Blue acted," she says. "He's been fighting him for a long time. Well, he's not going to do it again." I open the door for a last look as the gray pickup burns rubber down Quentin Road. "We better be extra careful around here for a while," she says. "Double-lock all the doors and keep our eyes and ears open, right?"

"Yes, ma'am," I reply. "I mean, Josie. Right."

TWENTY-EIGHT

Riding home, I'm thinking about, what else, the guy and his son who tried to steal Blue. After they left, I walked Blue around until he settled down. When I got back inside, Josie asked if I really wanted to adopt him. She said it was nice that I offered, but if I didn't mean it, he could stay at the shelter with her and Pal forever, no worries.

I told her I was pretty much sure from the first time I saw him. Now it was definite.

Josie complimented me on keeping my cool during the whole thing. I told her I was scared but didn't want to let on. "Besides," I said, "I've had some experience with someone else like that." I whistled, "Man, you really handled that guy." Josie said she had some experience with someone like that, too.

She told me about her ex-husband, Roy, and he sounded a lot like my father. Josie only hinted at the beatings, but she didn't need to draw me a picture. It seemed a lot like our house, but with no kids, so it was only her for this angry guy to take out all his problems on.

But not for long. When she learned that the cops and the courts wouldn't help, Josie called her cousin, a trooper with the state police.

She said that was funny because, when her cousin was younger, everyone figured he'd end up on the other side of the law. But he straightened himself out, got into law enforcement, and was the one guy in the family you called if you needed help. Like Josie did then.

Her cousin took a few days off from work and came for a visit. He put new locks on her doors and windows, slept on her couch while waiting for her ex-husband to show up, and bought her a present: a twelve-gauge shotgun. Then he took her out to the range and taught her how to use it.

When Josie's ex appeared a few nights later, trying his old key in the new lock, Josie greeted him with the twelve-gauge. Seems like Roy had a fear of weapons because he backed up to his car, muttering threats all the way there. That's where he ran into her cousin holding a baseball bat, who convinced him never to return. And he never did.

I lied about filling out an application for Blue. The person who tells me about the law tells me that there's lying and then there's perjury. I know what my mother would say: "A lie is a lie." And I know what Ray would say: "Last liar wins."

This time I'm with Ray.

The man lied when he said Blue was a family pet, that he never fought him, and that he didn't know where his scars came from. All lies. People already think I killed my father. Calling me a liar isn't going to hurt my reputation much.

But lying under oath is a different story. That's perjury and that's big trouble. If the judge catches you in one lie, he can decide everything you're telling him is a lie and drop the hammer on you.

I don't think the judge in my case is as dumb as some other people I can think of—Daryl, for instance—so I decide not to lie at the inquest, if I can avoid it.

Thinking about one bad habit, lying, leads me, for some reason, to thinking about another: fighting. Nobody will believe me, especially Ms. Lepton, but I want to stop; I'm just not sure how. Miller and I were talking about it one day, and I asked him how he never gets into any brawls. He lives in the Oaks like me, goes to the same school, hears the same trash talk, but he skates through life without a scratch.

Maybe it's because Miller's smaller, or smarter. Or when people see us together, they just figure I'm the one who's going to throw down. Or maybe nobody wants to deal with his older brother coming after them later. He told me it was none of those things. "So what is it, then?" I asked him.

"I don't care," he answered.

I told him I really wanted to know.

"Dummy, I just told you," he said. "I don't care."

Then he told me, "You're always ready to pound some kid because of something he said about you or your family. Me, I could care less."

I just stared at him, so he kept going.

Miller told me that he made a decision after his father killed himself. He figured things couldn't get any worse, so he decided why worry about all the mental defectives around here and whatever they think?

It seemed strange to hear that his father's suicide rocked his world that much. Even stranger to talk about it in his room with the Farrah Fawcett posters taped all over the walls and ceiling, but I knew what he meant. It's not like either of our fathers got sick and died in a hospital or an old folks' home.

And even though he and I both wished our fathers would disappear, neither of us expected it to happen. They both died young and all of a sudden. Usually, that means a work accident or behind the wheel of a car, but that wasn't the reason with Miller's father, or mine.

"Anyway," Miller said, "when I'm seventeen, I'm going to join the Marines and say the hell with Bent Oaks and everyone in it." I thought about that and started laughing.

"What's so funny?" he wanted to know.

"Now who's the dummy?" I said.

"What do you mean?"

"Well, I think the Marines are going to expect you to fight," I told him.

The trouble is that what works for Miller doesn't necessarily work for me. He's the thinker, and I'm the fighter. That's just the way it is. Some guys around here think that sounds pretty cool. It's not, though, because after every fight there's always someone new waiting to take a shot at you. Even when you win, you lose.

I can't show up to a challenge like the one with Teski the other day and say, "Sorry, dude, I've given up fighting and taken up bike racing. Good luck to you, though. Hey, want to go for a ride?" But maybe, just maybe, if I stopped caring?

I try to picture myself walking away from any of the guys I've traded punches with the last couple of years, especially if they taunt me into fighting.

Mr. Schmink always says, "If you believe it, you can achieve it." Well, I don't believe it. Not yet. Guess I'll just have to take Mr. Schmink's word on that one.

Pulling up to our trailer, I get off my bike and walk up slow and quiet. Standing there in the yard, I'm admiring our new fence and daydreaming about the next couple of weeks. There's only a few more days of school, and after that, a few more days until the coroner's inquest—I just might make it. Laughing out loud, I think, "If you believe it, you can achieve it."

Turning, I notice a neighbor lady walking past, but she hurries away when she sees me. Things haven't changed that much around here.

One thing that has changed, and I guess it's changing still, is my attitude. Lately, I'm thinking about all the people who want to know what happened that night. Maybe they should just ask me—maybe I'll tell them.

The rumor going around is that I flat-out executed my father. The person who told me about the law says that would be first-degree murder—pretty much impossible when someone dies during a fight. Either he fell and hit his head or someone smashed it in the heat of the moment. Hard to plan, and harder to prove.

Killing someone with poison? Now that's premeditated. You'd have to buy the poison somewhere secretly, slip it to your victim, then sit there and watch him basically melt from the inside out before you call an ambulance. Pretty cold-blooded. But a hit on the head during a fight? That's either manslaughter or self-defense.

Even my father's cop shows knew the difference between those.

I don't know how long I've been standing on the back porch. I look up and see Kyla through the kitchen window. For once, it's all quiet in Bent Oaks.

Then I remember that I don't have to be, quiet that is, and just to prove it, I go back down the four steps to my bike, pick it up, drop it hard against the porch, and then stomp up the stairs and fling open the back door—just to show that I can.

My sister jumps at the sound as I burst, laughing, into the kitchen. My mother's at the table, giving Kyla advice as she attempts another recipe. I check the stovetop to see what's cooking. "You must have had a good day," my mother says.

I tell her that it feels good to make some noise. Not like when I used to creep up to the house so I wouldn't upset him. "Him." Not Father and definitely not Dad. But she knows who I mean. "Crazy, right?"

"I don't think you're crazy," she says.

"You know," I tell her, "as far back as I can remember, I was always trying not to upset him. Until right at the end, I figured it out. Everything upset him and nothing was ever going to change."

My mother looks at me all mom-like and says, "Spence, I never asked, but I will, because you might want to talk about it, and if you don't, that's fine, but we can . . ."

"About the night it happened?" I ask.

"Yes, because you were there and maybe you're feeling some, I don't know, guilt, like there was something you could have done, and you shouldn't, but if you want to talk about anything . . ."

"I'm going to take a shower before dinner," I tell her, and I head off down the hallway.

TWENTY-NINE

Carl Washington is a gambler. He bets on card games, dice games, football, horse racing—just about any activity where money can be won, or lost. He's even grown to tolerate dogfighting, a "sport" he's been introduced to by his part-time boss, Jeremiah Lime.

Arriving home from the racetrack, Carl hears his phone ringing. Checking the number, he almost lets the call go to voice mail. But since he's lost races all day, is almost broke, and is two weeks overdue on the rent, he picks up. For better or worse, a call from Mr. Lime usually means a little money might be coming Carl's way.

Lime instructs Carl to find a new location for their Chicago dogfights. Some people are thrifty. Mr. Lime is cheap. Having lost Spike, at least temporarily, Lime isn't about to throw away more money by leaving his training supplies behind. Changing houses is one way to stay ahead of the authorities. The police don't show much interest in animals tearing each other to pieces but sometimes make trouble for squatters who take over empty properties.

Carl has performed this task before. Borrowing a truck and getting help from Javier, he'll move the bedroom doors that form the pit, along with the treadmill, medicines, and other supplies to a garage he rents until another vacant house can be found.

In truth, Carl sees Mr. Lime as nothing more than a paycheck. He takes Lime's money but hates to watch the dogfights. Carl thinks of his pet beagle, Buddy, whenever two dogs enter the ring, and never mentions to his wife where he's been on "fight nights."

Javier Rodriguez has no such concerns. He's traveled to Lime's farm to help out on several occasions, though leaving the city for the country makes him nervous.

On his last visit, Javi looked around at the endless wide-open spaces. The only thing that looked like it hadn't grown up out of the ground was a house on a distant hill. "How far away?" he wondered.

Javier is accustomed to city measurements: blocks, half blocks, the distance between bus stops and L stations. The house might have been a shack just up the hill or a mansion five miles away. He had no way of knowing.

Javi always enjoyed getting back home after these visits, especially when Lime's dogs had done well and his pockets were full.

Carl had planned to tell Lime of his "retirement" from dogfighting during their call today. Until his disastrous day at the racetrack.

Having lost the first few races, Carl doubled down on a "sure thing" in a later race. He bet all the money he had, five hundred dollars, on number five in the fifth race, liking all the fives in that bet. Hurrying to the finish line, he watched as his horse came in fifth. "That figures," he cursed as he tore up the losing ticket.

Now he has to stay with Lime for a little while longer. But one day soon he'll tell Lime what he really thinks of his dirty dogfighting business. Then Carl will return to a clean life of poker, crap games, parlays, and roulette.

Not that Lime will be terribly broken up by the news. Yes, there will be the usual trouble of finding a new helper in the city—a criminal he can trust. And he'll have to warn Carl not to discuss anything he's seen or heard while working together, but that's routine. If Carl is arrested on some other charge, he might be tempted to talk about Lime to keep himself out of jail.

But Carl, Lime, and the police all know that dogfighting is far down anyone's list of "serious crimes." So far down that there isn't anything Carl could tell the police about Lime that they would care to hear. Lime knows that helpers come and go. Some go to jail, some go straight, some die, and some like Carl have no stomach for the violence of the sport.

The same is true of the dogs. Some grow old, some come up lame, they all die, eventually, but still Lime carries on. At least he has a son to lean on.

Lime likes to think ahead three or four years. By then, Caleb will be running the farm while Lime works full-time with the dogs. Lime thinks of Caleb more as a business partner than a son. He knows nothing of his son's life—school activities, friends, grades—only that he's a first-rate dog trainer and a hard worker around the farm. All the others can come and go, but Lime would be lost without Caleb.

Funny, but it never occurs to him to say so.

THIRTY

Another day, another special project at the shelter. Today I'm "Farmer Spence," cleaning out the horse stalls and chicken coop. I've brought home eggs from the chickens a few times—not easy on a two-mile bike ride—so I guess it's only fair that I have to clean the coop once in a while.

Man, it stinks.

I've got a bandanna over my nose and mouth, and I'm counting the minutes until I'm done.

I'm also counting the hours, about two, until I can bring Blue home.

I wasn't planning on getting a dog before the inquest. It just worked out that way. Now, if something happens to me, my mother will have to take care of Blue. I probably should have waited, but I'm hoping Blue will bring me luck.

Besides, I keep thinking that the dogfighter and his son might come back some night to steal him. The sooner I get him out of the shelter, the better.

I was going to wait a month—until after the Fourth of July—because of what goes on around Bent Oaks at the holiday every year. I worry about the craziest things sometimes.

I'm remembering a couple of years ago, when this guy celebrated the Fourth by firing his rifle straight up into the air at midnight. What if he did that this year? The Oaks is a good place not to be on the holiday. People blow off fireworks all day, but it gets worse after dark.

Josie told me she usually spends that night in the kennel, trying to calm down dogs that are freaked out by the noise. This year, maybe Blue and I can join her.

I keep thinking about that guy and his rifle. Since his friends had fireworks and he didn't, he went and got his M1 and started shooting at the moon. The next morning, one of his neighbors found a bullet half buried in his kitchen floor. Trying to figure out where it came from, he pulled over a chair, stood on it, and had a look around. Finding a hole in his kitchen ceiling, he poked his little finger up through the roof to the outside.

If that bullet had come through above his bed instead of his kitchen, well, I guess he wouldn't have needed the chair.

How fast does a bullet fall after it flies straight up for about half a mile, then turns around and heads back to earth? Beats me, but it might make a good science fair project in a couple of years.

All I know is that our trailer is pretty much a thin layer of sheet metal with a little insulation between the walls and ceilings. So getting out of the house on a night when guns, M-80s, and cherry bombs are going off all over the neighborhood sounds like a good idea to me.

Josie's offered to drive me and Blue home after work today. Ray's there right now, putting up our mailbox. That reminds me of what I found the other day when Ray and I were finishing the fence: a letter from a dead man.

I was moving the mailbox, and inside I saw this official-looking letter for my mother.

I recognized the name on the return address right away: it was from a drinking buddy of my father's who also happened to be his lawyer. Even though it was addressed to my mother, I tore it up and threw it in the trash without reading it.

So right before he died my father had this lawyer draw up some sort of nasty surprise for my mother. Did he want a divorce, or child custody, or to take away the trailer? Who knows? Whatever it was, I'm sure it wasn't good. Even after he's gone, my father keeps trying to drop bad news on us.

My friend who knows about the law said the person who answers a lawsuit is called a "respondent." If my father's drunk lawyer friend wants our "response" to the letter, he can find it at the bottom of the trash can.

It's funny, but now that he's gone, I can see my father a lot more clearly. That sounds like something my uncle would say, but it's true.

When he was around every day, my father seemed almost normal, especially in Bent Oaks. Now, when I talk to someone like Mr. Schmink, or Josie, or Alicia's parents—even Ray when he's sober—it makes my father seem kind of like a maniac or something. And I guess he was.

Like, all the things those other people believe in, my father always laughed at. Things like getting out of the foundry, or going away to college, or having a career somewhere.

Suddenly, another random thought pops into my head. A lot of random thoughts appear when you're cleaning chicken crap. I guess it's to keep you from thinking about what you're actually doing.

The thought is that maybe I should start thinking more seriously about high school. Why? Because then I can think seriously about college.

If I ever go, and finish, I'll be the first in the family to do it. Something about shoveling horse manure and chicken droppings makes going to college sound like a not-too-bad idea. I have no idea what I want to be in life besides "not a manure shoveler," but I guess I've got a few years to work that out. I suppose finishing eighth grade would be a good first step up the educational ladder. In the meantime, I keep shoveling.

THIRTY-ONE

Back home, I show Blue around his new house. After sniffing everywhere, he ends up in the laundry room where I figure he'll smell his blankets and see his toys and settle right in. Wrong. The first thing he does is make a beeline for my bedroom where he runs around before jumping up on the bed.

When I push him off to the floor, he lifts his leg and starts to pee. I grab him and run for the backyard with Kyla racing ahead to open the door.

While Blue explores the yard, Kyla starts talking again. Out of nowhere, she asks if I'm going to graduate eighth grade. I tell her, yeah, what a dumb question, there's only four days left in the school year. She asks about Alicia. She wants to know if I'm going to juvenile hall. She talks about school and dogs and the neighborhood. It reminds me of how she used to be.

She asks if our mother will marry Daryl.

"Not a chance," I tell her.

"How do you know?"

"She's just being polite, like she is with everyone. Besides, if things get too bad, I'll fix it," I say.

"Like you fixed our other problem?" she asks.

I pretend not to hear her.

We chase Blue around his new yard, and he's loving it. I'm not worried about the peeing incident. I know Blue's housebroken. He's just been in the kennel too long. Before that, who knows how long the man kept him caged up with no bathroom breaks. I'll get him back on track. It just takes training.

Back inside, I clean the carpet, all the way down the hall and into my bedroom, with this cleaner we've got.

While I clean, I'm thinking about Kyla. "Fixed our other problem" could mean a lot of things, but I know my sister, and I know what she meant.

Sometimes I forget how Kyla watches everything. She sits quietly, listening to family fights and whispered discussions and policemen on the porch, and she takes it all in. She's smart. And she puts things together. Alicia, for instance. I never told Kyla about a girl at school, at least I don't think I did. But she knew about her. She knows what goes on around Bent Oaks and with my court case and with Daryl hanging around our trailer, and she must have some idea of what happened on "the night in question."

My little sister knows, or thinks she knows, what happened between my father and me on that final night.

That doesn't worry me at all.

Kyla only talks to people she likes, and she wouldn't like the judge or any of the other "professionals" assigned to my case. There's no one I'd trust to keep a secret more than her. That's the way it's always been in our family. And, at least for now, she doesn't know exactly what that secret is.

Blue's scratching at the door, so it's back outside again. Kyla's laughing and talking while Blue explores his new territory. When it gets quiet, I look up and see my sister slipping into the house and closing the door behind her. Then I see why. Daryl's heading our way.

Daryl reminds me of a movie bad guy—always showing up when you least expect him.

He strolls over and stares at the new fence. "Not bad," he says. He grabs a post and gives it a shake. After opening and closing the gate a few times, he nods at me like he's the local gate-checker and I just passed the inspection. "Better get a lock," he tells me.

"Hmm," I think. "Did Daryl just have a good idea?" I make a mental note to pick up a lock the next time I'm in town.

My mother, always one move behind in the game of Daryl, steps outside. If she'd waited a few more seconds, he might have been off to check on someone else's gate. Now she's stuck. I think she was coming out to play with Blue, and instead she has to deal with Daryl. Still, she does her polite thing and says hello.

I wonder how she'd feel if she had seen him creeping around our trailer with a flashlight a few nights ago.

Apparently, Daryl's out to break his own record for being annoying. He gets right to the point. "That's a dangerous-looking dog," he says. "Pit bull, isn't he?"

"He's a Staffordshire terrier," I tell him.

"Better be careful," he calls to my mom. "He'll attack someone and you'll be responsible." I'm thinking that if Blue was going to attack anyone it would have been the man and his son who tried to steal him, and all he did was try to hide.

I'm at the gate. Daryl's standing in the road. I whistle for Blue and he works his way over. Rubbing his neck and shoulders, I say, "How do you know he's no good if you don't give him a chance?" Blue looks up at Daryl, shy, but willing to make a friend.

"I just know," Daryl announces, crossing his arms across his chest.

I'm ready to argue with him, maybe even ask what he was doing outside our house at midnight with a flashlight, when I notice the way my mother's staring. Just that quickly she's made up her mind. She's had enough of Daryl.

I recognize that look from years ago. So many years that it's hard to remember now, but it's the same way she looked at my father when she finally gave up on him ever being a decent man.

If Daryl's the movie bad guy who jumps out unexpectedly, my mother's the hero who kills him with a sword or spear or silver bullet. Then the guy stares for a few seconds before he realizes he's dead, finally falling over all dramatic-like.

Daryl's dead and he doesn't even know it.

"Come inside, Spence," my mother calls, and lets the door slam behind her.

THIRTY-TWO

Yesterday, Blue and I went in and out of the yard about a hundred times and took three walks.

After dinner, I finished "dog-proofing" the house like I was supposed to do earlier but never got around to.

Basically, you get down on your hands and knees and find anything that a dog might chew up or swallow. Things like rubber bands, beer caps, or whatever, so I guess it's good my father always drank from cans and not bottles. Blue's not a puppy, so I don't expect him to be a chewer, but you never know.

On one of my trips coming in from the yard, I pranked Kyla by calling out in my best "Daryl" voice, "Kyla, have you learned about the Constitution yet, and can you tell me about it?" She was sitting on the couch with her back turned. I knew I got her though, because her neck tensed up and she jumped half out of her chair before she turned around and saw it was me.

We both cracked up. Kyla did her Daryl imitation, followed by another one of mine. That's when my mother walked into the room and said, "Maybe we don't need to hear that person's name around here anymore." And she wasn't joking. Bravo, Mother.

There's four days remaining until the end of the school year. Right now that feels like a long time. Classes don't bother me; it's the in-betweens that I worry about. Walking the halls, lunch period, getting to and from school. That's when trouble happens, if it's going to happen.

As for lunch, I've been splitting my days between Alicia's table and the guys from the Oaks. The Bent Oaks table is the loudest, and the one that Mr. Sullivan keeps the closest eye on. I know I'm playing with fire, but these are the guys I know and have to live with, so I still spend some time with them.

As far as fighting, there's three guys for sure I have to watch out for: Teski, Sulieman, and Roselli. If any of them wants to start something, he's got less than a week to do it. Personally, I'd like to round up all three of them for a one-time, winner-take-all grudge match and get it over with.

"And what would that solve?" I can almost hear Mr. Schmink asking. "Nothing" is what I'm supposed to answer. But I don't feel that way. It's just something I say because it sounds good to people like Mr. Schmink or Ms. Lepton or the judge.

Speaking of fights, there was another one in the Oaks last night. Some guy and his wife were duking it out about a block west of our place, near Miller's trailer. The sound carried all the way into our living room. It went on so long that the cops showed up. The guy was still screaming from the back seat of the squad car as it pulled away. Business as usual.

It was tough leaving Blue at home this morning. But I got lucky. My mother's working the dinner shift tonight, so she'll be home with him while I'm at school. I'm pulling into the school parking lot when I see Alicia. I catch her at the front door and we walk inside together to start another day.

THIRTY-THREE

Wednesday after school, I stop by Ray's house on my way to the shelter. I knock on the door and he answers right away. He's hanging cabinets in the kitchen, and he looks sweaty and healthy.

Healthier, I guess.

He's still super thin, and he's breathing hard, but his eyes are clear. I notice right away because he looks me in the eye when he shakes my hand. I can't remember him ever doing that before.

I tell Ray I just stopped by to say thanks for working on the fence. He asks about Blue. Then he tells me it's an anniversary, that he hasn't had a drink for seven days. I tell him I've only got two more days of school and six until the inquest. Ray says that calls for a drink and leads me to the kitchen.

He pours me a glass of lemonade from a pitcher on the counter. Not the kind from a carton, but fresh squeezed. It's cold and good. I think about asking him how he gave up drinking alcohol, but it seems too personal, so I don't.

I wonder if my father ever tried. I can't remember him ever talking about it, or going even a single day without, so probably not. Ray clinks my glass with his. I hang around, holding a couple of cabinets steady while he screws them into the wall, and after a while we head out to the garage to get more screws.

I ask my uncle if he has any spare locks lying around. "I've got one of everything out here," he says. "The trick is finding it." He digs around in a stack of boxes full of nuts and bolts and tools and faucets and doorknobs until he pulls out a combination lock. He twirls the numbers and it pops right open.

"My birthday," he says, "but you can change it if you like."

Back inside, we hang another cabinet and Ray tries the door. It swings nice and easy. "Just like the gate," I say. Ray puts down his screwdriver and looks around at his old house, saying, "Thought I might fix this place up."

Noticing the peeling paint, chipped floors, and sagging doors, I think, "Good luck with that."

Catching the look on my face, Ray laughs and says, "Well, it might take a while."

I smile and say, "Hey, if you believe it, you can achieve it."

"Where the heck did you hear that?" he asks.

I tell my uncle I've got to get to the shelter. He seems kind of sad when he says, "Used to be, whenever I finished a day's work, first thing I'd do was have a drink."

Finally, he picks up his glass and says, "Well, lemonade's a drink, right?" and he drains it dry.

He's pouring us each another when his telephone rings. He's not saying much into the phone, just "uh-huh" and "okay," before he finally turns to me and says, "You better get home."

THIRTY-FOUR

Back home, the gate's open and our house is empty. Blue's leash is missing, so I figure Kyla's got him out for a walk. I get back on my bike to have a look around.

A block from home I can hear my sister's voice. I try to figure out how far away she is and in which direction. I'm guessing she's over near Miller's place, like the screaming couple from two nights earlier.

When I find her, Kyla's crying and calling for Blue. She has his leash in her hand and tells me he got out of the yard somehow. "But he's only been gone about fifteen minutes, so he's got to be close by."

I start out by shouting, "Who left the gate open?" but Kyla says when she put Blue in the yard, the gate was closed. In my pocket, I can feel the weight of Ray's lock. I kick at the ground, angry with myself for waiting so long to lock the gate.

We split up to look around the Oaks.

I take off on my bike while my sister keeps going on foot. When I circle back ten minutes later, Kyla hasn't seen anything and neither have I. She tells me she called our mother at work and I look up and see the station wagon cruising toward our trailer.

I follow every east-west street in the Oaks asking people if they've seen a dog, then do the same on the north-south streets. Finally, I get off my bike and walk the same ground again, calling out Blue's name as I go.

After an hour of searching, Ray shows up. It's dinnertime when we head out again. Long after we called them, I see a cop car pulling in. It's the sergeant from the night my father died. Pedaling back to meet him in front of our trailer, I try to tell him everything all at once, but he mostly ignores me and talks to my mother. He writes down Blue's description, but doesn't seem interested in doing anything else.

"The gate was open. He'll come back when he gets hungry," the sergeant keeps repeating. I tell him the gate was closed, but it's no use. He gets a call on his radio about some other trouble nearby and takes off in a hurry. He isn't anything like the police on my father's TV shows, that's for sure.

After he leaves, we grab some flashlights and try again. Kyla stays home with the outdoor lights on and the doors locked. She promises to check the yard every few minutes to see if Blue shows up. Then my mother, my uncle, and I walk every inch of the Oaks. After that, we hop in the car and drive the back roads nearby, shining our flashlights and calling Blue's name as we go.

It's late when we finally get back home. Looking shook up and scared, Kyla heads off to bed without saying a word. I believe her when she says she closed the gate—but I also want to know how Blue managed to escape. As soon as we get him back, I'm locking the gate and keeping it that way.

I can't sit still. I'm pacing back and forth from the yard to the laundry room to the front window, until my mother finally tells me to sit down and relax. She says if I settle down, she'll help me design a "Missing Dog" poster that we can hang copies of around town tomorrow. We sit at the kitchen table with some blank typing paper and markers and a photo of Blue and get to work.

THIRTY-FIVE

The next morning, I hear Ray moving around in the kitchen. I'm glad he stayed over because coffee sounds like a good idea, and I can smell a pot brewing. I get cleaned up quick and join him at the table. After a few sips of caffeine, I grab the poster for the copy shop. My mother's voice stops me as I reach for the doorknob. "I'll drop that off on my way to work," she says.

"I'm taking it over now," I tell her.

"Before school?" she asks. "You'll be late."

"I'm not going to school," I say. "I'm going to have the guy make fifty copies, then hang them around town while I look for Blue."

She tells me I'll be in trouble at school. I tell her there's only two days left. "I've taken all my tests, and, besides, they're already sending me to summer school, what else can they do to me? They can't suspend me now."

I don't mention the judge's warning to be in class every minute of every day until the end of the school year. But if my mother's not going to bring it up, neither am I.

"How are you going to pay for the copies?" she wants to know, and she shoots a nasty look at her brother. But I didn't get the money from Ray. I've got a hundred-dollar bill in my pocket courtesy of the dogfighter. Ever since that day, I've been expecting him to stop by the shelter and demand his money back. But he hasn't. So too bad. If he ever comes back, I'll give him his hundred minus the cost of the copies.

Or maybe I won't. I'm not too worried about some old dogfighter and his money, especially if he got it by betting on two dogs tearing each other to pieces.

Just then, Kyla shuffles down the hall, looking all guilty about last night. "Don't worry," I tell her. "We'll have Blue back by tonight."

I know my mother has to get Kyla on her bus and get herself to work. Glaring at me, she asks again, "Are you going to school or not?"

"Not," I say before hustling out the back door and hopping on my bike.

"Spence, come back here" is the last thing I hear as I pedal toward Halvdale, searching for Blue as I go.

Last night, I put together a poster with a description of Blue, our address and phone number, and a Polaroid I took of him on Sunday. Ray said to add a fifty-dollar reward because most people wouldn't bother calling without it.

"Put it on top where people can see it," he added.

Then he walked over to the couch, took off his shoes, lay down, and fell asleep in about five seconds.

Before I went to bed, I checked the yard one last time. I unlatched the gate and left the back door open before rolling out my sleeping bag on the laundry room floor. I thought it would be hard to sleep out there, but it wasn't.

I know I'm taking a chance by skipping school. Just being on the street during class hours could get me picked up by the truant officer. But a couple of the private schools are already done for the year, so I'm probably safe.

Besides, I have to look for Blue. There's no way I can sit in class all day wondering where he is. If I'm lucky, I'll have him back by tonight. If Ray has to give someone fifty dollars to make it happen, that's what we'll do. I'll pay him back out of the dogfighter's money, if I have to. Right now, I just want my dog back.

I ride along calling for Blue all the way out of the Oaks and into Halvdale.

Would he wander this far from home? Maybe. But then I get an idea of somewhere else he might go: the shelter. It's eight thirty. I'm almost to the print shop, so I stop and check their hours: nine to five. I decide to bike over to Josie's.

Pedaling down Quentin Road, I see buses full of kids heading to various schools.

I think about Alicia and what she'll think when I don't show up today. Pretty soon, the shelter comes into view. I walk around the entire property before knocking on the door.

Josie's in the kennel doing the cleaning, and I tell her about Blue disappearing from our yard. I ask her if she's seen anything and she says no, but she'll keep her eyes open and wishes me luck.

Back in town, I pass a line of cars waiting to buy gas; there's been a shortage ever since the economy went bad. Now you have to fill up on odd or even days depending on your license plate number. Trying to cut the line, a guy in a red sports car almost runs me over.

My reflectors don't help. I guess they'll run over a kid on a bike even in the daytime around here.

The print shop is just opening. I tell the man behind the counter that I've got a rush job. "Rush jobs cost extra," he tells me. That doesn't sound good. But when I show him the paper with all the info and the picture of Blue, he says, "You lost your dog? That's too bad." Then he asks if I have any money.

"You bet," I say, and pull out the hundred. He holds the bill up to the light and turns it over, studying both sides.

"Is this real?" he asks.

"Yeah," I say, although actually I have no idea. After looking at the hundred through a magnifying glass, he tells me he'll start my job right away.

"It'll take an hour and cost ten dollars."

I'm back home by four in the afternoon. I spent the day calling for Blue and hanging posters with a roll of tape and a staple gun the print guy loaned me. I'm hungry and thirsty and out of posters, except for one copy that I saved to make more for tomorrow.

I call Josie to say I'll be late and ask if she's seen Blue. She tells me she hasn't seen anything and to just go ahead and take the day off; she'll see me tomorrow.

There's nothing to do now but wait. Wait to see if Blue shows up, or if anyone calls to claim the reward. My mother comes home with Kyla, who runs to her room without saying hello or even asking about Blue. Just when I thought she was getting better, this happens, and I wonder if she's going to stop talking again.

Ray stops by and slaps two twenties and a ten on the table. "I'm feeling optimistic," he says. "Someone will call to say they found him, wait and see."

My mother isn't talking to me, except to say it won't do us any good to starve, and she starts dinner. I'm trying to help by chopping vegetables, but my mother calls to Kyla, "Honey, come out here and show your brother how it's done."

Ray and I talk about where I searched today, and he asks if the lock I borrowed was for the new gate. I tell him it's probably the only good idea Daryl ever had. If I had used it earlier, maybe Blue would still be here. Kyla's standing at the cutting board, going through the motions of helping to cook, when she starts to cry. My mother goes to her and says, "It's all right, sweetie. We'll get him back."

Kyla says, "I looked out the window and he was there, and when I looked again, he was gone."

"You saw Blue and then you didn't?" my mom asks.

Kyla just nods and cries a little more, and then adds, "And Daryl too."

I jump so high I practically hit the ceiling. "Daryl was there when Blue disappeared?" I ask. Kyla nods again.

"Honey, why were you looking just then?" my mom asks.

"I always look when I see Daryl, to make sure he's not coming to our door."

"Did Daryl have Blue?" I hold my breath waiting for her reply.

"No, he was just walking, and then a truck passed him and they were both gone."

Not much help in a neighborhood with so many of them, but I have to ask: "What kind of truck?"

Kyla just stares at the ground, and I know what that means. It means she's finished talking for a while. At least, I hope it's only a while and not months like the last time. Then she surprises me by clearing her throat and saying, "A gray pickup, with a sticker on the back. I never saw it before."

I have a crystal-clear picture of that truck in my mind. I can see it now fishtailing out of Josie's driveway and turning south on Quentin Road. A gray pickup with a bumper sticker reading "Farm Use", or "Farm USA" or something like that.

And I can still see the driver, shouting threats as his son opens the door and pushes him behind the steering wheel of that same truck. That's when I realize I really don't know anything about him—except for his plate number.

While Ray is telling Kyla what a good job she did, I pick up the phone. I don't usually say my prayers, but I try one now. Josie's phone rings five times with no answer. That means she's out in the kennel catching up on all the work I should be doing. I'm about to dial again, but instead I hang up and race for the front door.

"I'll be back," I shout as I run outside and jump on my bike.

With all the biking I've been doing lately, I can cover the distance to the shelter in ten minutes. On the way over, I argue with myself about whether it's right to ask God to help me, when I never talk to Him any other time. Then I think about Josie's desk piled high with folders, receipts, and clippings.

What are the odds she still has the guy's license number? Not very good, I'm thinking.

That's when I decide to ask for His help "just this once." I know that's what everyone says, except for people who pray all the time, but maybe I can use some of their built-up prayers for something like this. As I pull into her driveway, I see Josie walking back from the kennel to her house.

"Just this once," I say out loud.

THIRTY-SIX

The previous night, Blue found himself bouncing along in a cramped cage in the back of Jeremiah Lime's pickup truck. He didn't need to be told his destination—or his fate. Soon, he would be returning to his old routine of running on a treadmill, pulling a heavy sled around the hot, dusty yard, and engaging in tune-up fights.

Blue's life, and his name, had changed when he was found in the house in the city. The young man who found him brought him to the place with other dogs run by the woman. He was beginning to believe that there were good humans in the world when the boy, Spence, became his friend.

After that, the bad man and his son came back, twice. On their second visit, they took Blue from Spence's yard and drove him back to the only real home he's ever known. The one with rusty crates, training pits, and faraway fights, where some dogs come home alive and others don't.

Today, Blue and the other dogs are "chained out" around the yard. Close enough to see and hear are others like himself, secured to tractor tires or stakes driven into the earth. With no food, water, or shade from the hot sun, the dogs flatten to the ground and pant and wait.

Blue doesn't understand why he can't run free, or be close enough to the other dogs to form a pack and become friends. Can't understand so much about this strange place and the bad man who controls every detail of the dogs' lives here.

Blue's father, Dig, had been one of the bad man's most successful fighters. The man had forced him to fight at least half a dozen times a year for five years. In his final fight, Dig's heart gave out at the end of a two-hour match. Even though he'd given his life for the man, Dig was tossed into the burial pit without a second thought. Later, he was cursed by the man, who had lost money on the fight.

Blue doesn't know any of that, of course. All he knows, right now, is that he misses Spence.

The boy here looks a little like Spence in size and age, but he isn't the same. Sometimes, this boy looks at him the way Spence did, but only when the bad man isn't around. Whenever the bad man appears, the boy tenses up and Blue senses that he is as afraid of the man as the dogs are.

The man frightens Blue, as well, and he does his best to please him, although nothing he does, or doesn't do, seems to matter. The man always treats the dogs the same way: cruelly.

Life here is one long cruelty.

Blue is starved, or beaten, or taken to training sessions where the dogs are forced to tear into each other—for what reason, Blue isn't sure. Once, he thought he was free. He had gone to sleep in the cold, dark house, hoping never to awaken.

But a dog's life is one of chance. By chance, Blue was found by the young man, who brought him to the woman, who introduced him to Spence. He remembers his mother, who taught him to never give up. He thinks that if he can get away from this place and these two humans, maybe he can find his way back to Spence. Or that maybe, somehow, Spence will find his way to him.

THIRTY-SEVEN

When I ask Josie if she has the paper with the guy's plate number, she walks to her desk and stares. After a few seconds she reaches into the middle pile of paperwork, leafs down about halfway, and plucks it out. I ask her why she saved it, along with all the other junk that piles up around the shelter, and she says, "I'm thorough." I thank her about five times, then reach out to grab the paper.

"Wait a minute," she says. "You don't want to lose that."

Josie takes the paper from my hand, copies the number onto another sheet of paper, hands me the original, and puts the copy back in the same spot in the middle pile. Thorough.

The ride back takes forever. I pedal along thinking that once I give the cops the guy's plate number, they'll race right over and arrest him. I'll probably have

Blue back by morning. I forget about thanking God now that I've got what I want, so I guess I'm like everyone else in that way. But I promise not to ask Him for anything else—for a while, anyway. That sounds like everyone else too.

Back home, I drop my bike in the yard, run inside with the piece of paper, and yell, "You can call the cops. I know who took Blue."

Ray grabs the phone and dials. After that, things come to a dead stop.

The police say they'll send a patrol car in the morning, not tonight. Ray tries to reason with them, saying they don't need to send a car, that he'll read them the number over the phone, or we can drive over to the station. They don't care. It seems they'd do more about a missing bike than a missing dog.

It's tough to sit around and wait for morning, but what can I do? Blue didn't run away, so looking around here won't help. I know who has him, but who is he, exactly? Ray thinks the Department of Motor Vehicles might look up a number for us, but they're closed until tomorrow anyway.

It seems like the last couple of days have caught up with me because suddenly I'm dead tired. I put my head down on the kitchen table—to rest for a minute—and a minute later I'm fast asleep.

My mother wakes me with a plate of food. While we eat, Ray keeps chatting up Kyla, but it's no use; she just stares at her plate for most of the meal. After dinner, I dial Alicia. I fill her in on Blue disappearing and what I've been up to, and then I hand the phone to my sister.

Something tells me Kyla will open up to Alicia even when she won't talk to me. A minute later she's telling Alicia about her life at school, and the Oaks, and all the details on some new boy she likes from Halvdale. Who knew?

I'm looking out the window, half listening, when a movement outside catches my eye. It's Daryl.

I'm out the door in record time. Running through the open gate, I head straight for him.

Daryl must know something's wrong because he turns away, picking up his pace. "Wait a minute," I yell. Catching up, I ask him if he was around when Blue disappeared.

"I was wondering why your gate was open," he says, and just stands there grinning.

"I asked you a question," I say.

He answers slowly, still wearing that same stupid grin. "I told you to get a lock," he says.

That's when I lose it.

I remember throwing punches, lots of them. Daryl's trying to cover up, but at least one gets through. I can feel his nose crack under my knuckles and there's blood everywhere. Is he trying to fight back and not very good at it? Or just protecting himself? I'm not sure because just like the bad guys on my father's cop shows, everything happens so fast that I can't remember it all. The next thing I know, we're on the ground. I'm on top, throwing more punches before Ray and a neighbor pull me off.

After he climbs to his feet, Daryl says I'm crazy and he doesn't know anything about my stupid dog. Then he spits out some blood and says, "I told you he was no good."

I lunge for him again and Ray can't hold me back, but the cop sure can. It's the cop from "the night in question," the young, strong one. I didn't hear him pull up or get out of his car, but I can feel his grip on my arms. He pins me against our new fence, looks me in the eye, and says, "Calm down right now, you got it?"

He follows that with "I'm gonna let go, and if you go after him again, you'll spend the night in jail."

I've seen lots of guys in the Oaks taken away in the back seat of a squad car, and I know he isn't bluffing. I nod okay, and he takes a slow step backward, keeping his eyes on me the whole time. Daryl starts to say something and the cop says, "Shut up, sir."

Noticing the open gate, he asks, "Does this have something to do with the dog?" I nod that it does, then the cop looks at Daryl and asks, "What's he got to do with it?"

"Ask him," I snap.

Turning to Daryl, he says, "Well?"

"Am I allowed to talk now?" Daryl answers like a whiny kid. The cop just stares until Daryl finally mumbles something about my dog running away and he doesn't know anything about it.

"He knows," I say. "He was here when my dog disappeared!"

The cop asks Daryl if that's true, and he sticks to his story. "Like I said before, I don't know anything."

Turning back to me, the cop asks, "How do you know he was here? Did you see him?" I tell him no, I didn't see him myself, but someone else did. "Who was that?" he wants to know. From the corner of my eye, I can see Kyla peeking out from behind the living room curtains. She looks about as scared as I've ever seen her. "Just a neighbor," I say.

The cop looks from me to Daryl, and then back again. "One doesn't know, and the other won't tell." Staring at Daryl, he says, "Sir, do you want to press charges against this—boy?" I can hear Ray laughing behind me.

Daryl looks around: at me, at the neighbors watching from their porches, at Ray, and finally at my mother. "No," he says.

The cop takes down Daryl's name and address, he already knows mine, and tells everyone else to "stop gawking and go on home." Before he leaves, he calls my mother over and says, "I don't want to come back here again tonight."

"Well, you should have come earlier when we called you," she answers, and presses the piece of paper with the license plate number into his hand.

She follows me back into our trailer, followed by Ray. Behind us, the cop swings the gate closed. I hear the metal click of the latch, and I'm glad that it's only a gate and not a cell door.

THIRTY-EIGHT

I had another dream last night. But it's not the dream I'm remembering, it's the waking-up part I can't seem to forget. Something strange happened when I sat up in bed and saw myself in the mirror above the dresser. I wasn't posing for a class picture or pretending to be someone else. I was just staring at my own half-awake reflection.

Right then, I could see myself the way the rest of the world sees me—"another Bent Oaks troublemaker."

The only thing Daryl was ever right about, besides the lock, was that most people think Bent Oaks people are no good. So it isn't just me. I'm not sure that helps much, though.

Mr. Schmink says it doesn't matter where you're from. His favorite line is "Just be yourself, Spence." Well, last night I was. I was more myself than

I've been in a long time. I grew up in a place where adults hit kids all the time, and sometimes—like me and Daryl last night—kids hit adults. People around town already think I'm a bully and I'm no good, and they're right. I could see it in the eyes of the people watching from their windows and porches: "It runs in the family."

Now I'm getting my own police file. Pretty soon it'll be thicker than my school file and I'll fit right in around here.

When I'm old enough, I can sit on the porch drinking beer, complaining about life, and when I get tired of that, I can head over to the junkyard for parts for my broken-down truck.

Mr. Schmink tries, but he's using Halvdale rules for Bent Oaks people. Like when he says I don't care what people think. I pretend I don't, but then I try to impress people like Josie or Alicia's family or anyone else outside of Bent Oaks.

I tried it and it didn't work.

I shouldn't be daydreaming about girls from nice families or moving out or going away to college because none of it's going to happen, ever.

Things never change around here. They just go in circles. Years ago, just up the road from our trailer, my mom and Ray were little kids dreaming about getting out of Bent Oaks one day.

They're still here.

Now it's Kyla and me, and I don't think the odds are any better for us than they were for them. There's only one thing I know for sure and that is—good or bad, Halvdale or Bent Oaks, student or dropout—I want my dog back.

Last night, I hit Daryl and I'm not sorry. When I find the guy who took Blue, I'll hit him the same way. I learned a few things from my father, like how to hit and how to take a hit and how to feel trouble coming by that electric tingle in the air when something bad is about to happen. All of that can come in pretty handy out there in the world.

I saw the look in Daryl's eyes when I caught up to him. He hoped I was bluffing, right until I landed the punch that broke his nose. I saw the same look on the man's face when Josie pulled the shotgun on him. I like that look. That's the way the guy and his son are going to look when I find them and take Blue back.

Tap, tap. There's a knock on my bedroom door, not too loud, but it shakes me up and I yell, "What!" When I open the door, Kyla's hurrying away down the hall.

Great. I'm sitting here having all these big revenge daydreams and, so far, the only one I'm scaring is my little sister.

I walk into the kitchen. My mother's getting ready to drop Kyla at Loraine's, then head to work. She says she'll drive me to school. "I'm not going," I tell her.

"I'm taking you, whether you want to go or not."

"I'll just walk home," I say.

So far, this morning feels like a replay of yesterday. I don't think my mother's even mad anymore, just worn out. She surprises me by picking up the phone and calling me in sick. "That will keep the truant officer away from our house for the day. I can't afford to leave work and bail you out," she says. And then she and Kyla grab their stuff and walk out the door.

I decide to wait until nine o'clock, "banker's hours" as Ray calls them, before calling the cops and asking about the plate number.

All alone in the house, I wander from room to room.

I think about Alicia and Miller and everyone else celebrating the last day of school. I walk in and out of the yard, through the laundry room, and back to the kitchen, where I make a pot of coffee. I try to think of a plan, but there is no plan. Either the cops have the guy's name and address or they don't. What am I supposed to do, roam the state asking people if they've seen my dog?

Just then, I look out the window and see a cop car pulling to a stop in front of our trailer. My bad morning just got worse. I figure that Daryl woke up and saw his black eyes and swollen nose and decided to press charges. That sounds like Daryl. I think about running out our back door and past Miller's place all the way to the highway, but then what?

The cop knows where I live, and he's got all the time in the world. He can stop back every day until he finally nabs me. I could roam the state looking for Blue, but five minutes ago that seemed like a dumb idea; it doesn't sound any smarter now.

The cop beeps his horn, so I walk out the front door and across the yard, wondering what's going to happen next. "Morning," he says.

It's the sergeant from the night in question, and he's smiling, sort of. "Have a good night?" he asks.

"Not really," I mumble.

"I heard." The sergeant leans into his car and grabs a piece of paper from a clipboard on the seat. He pauses a few seconds before reading from the paper. "We ran the plate number your mother gave us.

No luck." No luck? Was the guy not living where his license said, or was it a stolen car or something?

"What does that mean?" I ask.

The sergeant tells me there's no such plate number. He checked it himself, twice. "Sorry, kid, if there was such a number, we'd have a record of it."

My mind's spinning, and not just from surprise that the sergeant isn't here to arrest me. I wonder if maybe I called out the wrong number, or Josie wrote it down wrong. Either way, it doesn't exist.

So that's it, there's nowhere to look. Or there's everywhere to look, but not an address on a street in a town where I can pull up and find Blue and bring him back home.

The sergeant drives off.

Reaching the end of our road, he pulls a U-turn and heads back my way, looking straight ahead as he drives past.

I can't sit still, so I decide to take a ride. I look at the "Missing Dog" posters I hung up two days ago and scan the streets for a glimpse of Blue, but I know it's hopeless. After a while, I head for Josie's place.

It's not my regular time, and she may not even want me, but to be honest, I've got nowhere else to go. Besides, she's probably behind in her chores with me being off lately, so I keep on pedaling.

I'm embarrassed to show up without calling or anything, but when I knock on the door, Josie welcomes me inside. She asks about Blue, but when I tell her I don't want to talk about it, she just smiles and says she understands.

She goes back to her phone calls and paperwork, and I head out to the kennel where the dogs are glad to see me, and I'm glad to see them.

Working helps the time go by, and for a while I forget about everything. A few hours later, when I finish all the cleaning and feedings, I'm feeling better. When I go back to the house to ask about the walking schedule, there on the couch is Pal.

Seeing Pal feels like old times, and I just sit there on the couch, scratching his neck. I don't know if I've been there a few seconds or a few minutes, but the next thing I hear is Josie calling my name.

She asks about Blue, and I give her some of the story.

She asks again, so I give her the rest, from when he first disappeared right up to this morning when the cops told me they couldn't find the guy's plate number.

"Couldn't find his number?" Josie repeats. "How can that be?"

I tell her I don't know, that maybe we got the number wrong, but there's no such plate number on file. At least, that's what the cop said.

Josie makes a beeline for the desk and fishes out the paper with the guy's information on it. "Of course they don't have a record of it in Illinois. It's an Indiana license plate," she practically shouts at me. "See where I wrote *IN* next to the number?"

"Indiana," I repeat, like an idiot.

"You didn't have the wrong number," she tells me. "You got the wrong state."

She's all excited. "You have to call the police and tell them about this," she says. I get excited, too, until I remember that my mother and I have already pestered the Halvdale cops about three times for help. I don't think they're all sitting around just waiting to hear from either one of us again, especially me.

Josie can tell from the look on my face that something's wrong. I've never told her much about my father, besides him being a bad guy. And she for sure doesn't know about all the times Halvdale PD had been out to our trailer because he was busting the place up.

I also conveniently forgot to mention my fight with Daryl last night, so there's that, too.

"Something happened," I hear myself say.

That reminds me of Mr. Shmink and his "these things don't just happen" comment, so I decide to tell the truth. "I thought this guy in the neighborhood had something to do with Blue disappearing. I hit him, and the cops were there. It was kind of a mess," I say.

Josie stares at me a long time, like maybe she doesn't know me as well as she thought she did. That doesn't make me feel any better, but a few seconds later, she stops staring and reaches for her phone. "Spencer, I think we both know who took your dog, and you called the wrong cop."

I sit with Pal while Josie tries to get in touch with her cousin, the state trooper. When she can't reach him at work, she calls a number that he gave her for emergencies. After leaving a message, she paces the room for a minute, walking and thinking.

I can tell she's out of ideas when she says, "Why don't you start walking the dogs? I'll be in here working, and I'll let you know as soon as I hear something."

An hour ago, I thought there was no chance of finding Blue. Now there is, a slim one.

I plan on walking the dogs four at a time, figuring that way I'll be ready when her cousin calls. Ready for what? I guess, as Ray would say, "We'll burn that bridge when we get there."

"Don't worry, you'll find him," Josie tells me as I turn for the kennel. That's what I thought that first night Blue went missing, but, for some reason, this time I believe it.

An hour and a half later, I can't wait any longer. I burst into the house and ask Josie if she's heard anything yet. That's when something odd happens: she turns away, slides a piece of paper into the second pile on her desk, turns back around, and says, "No, nothing yet." All with the strangest look on her face.

I've seen that look before.

It's the same one my mother had when Kyla and I were kids and she'd cover up for our father. Like how he was "sick" when he really had a hangover. Or how he "got hurt at work" when he broke his hand punching a hole in one of our walls. Until she finally gave up because we never believed her anyway.

Apparently, Josie's as bad of a liar as my mother.

Not that I blame either one of them.

Nice people don't lie very often, so they're not good at it. Adults usually think they're doing a kid a favor if they keep something from them "for their own good." They figure it's easier to lie than to tell the truth about something bad.

Now Josie changes the subject. Telling me she's headed over to the diner to pick up lunch, she asks if I'd like anything. Only she doesn't say "the diner," she says "EAT." That's what the locals call the place, on account of the neon sign out front that flashes *E A T*.

"Sure, thanks," I say. "Just don't tell my mother it's for me. She might put some poison in it." Then I stand there alone as Josie and Pal pull out of the driveway and head into town.

For as long as I've been at the shelter, I've never snooped into anything I shouldn't. Never gone through the papers on the desk. Never listened in on a phone call. Never even opened the medicine cabinet in the bathroom.

I stare at the second pile of paperwork on the desk until the blood is pounding in my temples.

Stepping closer to the desk, I tell myself, "Just one look. If it's not what I think it is, I'll go right back to work."

I reach into the pile of papers and find the note I'm looking for. It's Josie's handwriting, but sloppy, like she wrote it in a hurry. It's a man's name and address: Jeremiah K. Lime, RR 3 BOX 96, Seven Hills Road, Clarkson, Indiana. With the out-of-state address, that's got to be him.

I memorize the address, but then I'm afraid I'll forget it, so I copy it on a second piece of paper and slide the first piece back into the pile. Thorough.

Why would Josie lie to me about her cousin calling back with Lime's address? The only reason I can figure is, he told her to wait. So the Illinois state trooper has time to call the Indiana troopers, who'll call the cops in the county where Lime lives, who might finally stop by his house one day and ask if he knows anything about a missing dog from Illinois.

And Lime will say, "No, I don't know what you're talking about." Meanwhile, they don't want some dumb kid to mess up their investigation. And by the time anyone gets around to doing anything about it, Blue could be dead.

A few minutes later, Josie cruises back down Quentin Road. She waves to me while I'm walking the last of the dogs. I see her but don't wave back.

I'm too distracted thinking about Jeremiah Lime from Clarkson, Indiana, and how I'm going to spend the first day of my summer vacation.

THIRTY-NINE

The next morning, a Friday, begins like yesterday and the day before. My mother's working the day shift at the diner. She sticks her head into my room to tell me the day's plan. I'm to watch Kyla until noon, then take her over to Loraine's before heading to work at the shelter.

I'm lying under the covers, fully dressed.

Hearing the front door close, I get up and make some coffee. I lay out all my paperwork: maps of Illinois and Indiana, train schedules, bus schedules, and Jeremiah Lime's address. From the laundry room, I take my backpack, Blue's leash, and a bag of dog treats.

The backpack hasn't been used in a while and I pull out a moldy sandwich and throw it in the trash. Walking from room to room, I grab a sweatshirt, a canteen, some extra socks, a toothbrush, and the ninety dollars left over from Mr. Lime's hundred.

I sit down to write a note while I sip my coffee. Without thinking it through, I scribble on a blank sheet of paper, "Dear Mom, I'm going to get Blue. I'll be back late tonight or tomorrow. Try not to worry. Spence." I'm about to tear that one up and start over when Miller appears over my shoulder.

"Boo!" he shouts.

"Damn, don't you ever knock?"

"I did," he says. "Guess you were too wrapped up in your homework to hear me. Didn't you get the memo? School's out, dude." Miller looks over my shoulder and catches on pretty quick that I'm not doing homework. "Takin' a trip?" he asks.

I scowl at him. "Why are you up so early?"

"I don't know," he says. "All year I've got to get up at the crack of dawn. Now it's vacation and I can't sleep."

"I know where Blue is and I'm going to get him," I tell him.

He lets out a low whistle. "What about the cops?" he asks.

"They already know, and they're not doing much about it, far as I can see."

Picking up the piece of paper with Lime's address scribbled on it, Miller reads out loud, "'Seven Hills Road, Clarkson, Indiana.'" He laughs. "Ridin' your bike all that way?"

Maybe it does sound crazy, but that's only because he doesn't know my plan. Last night, I mapped out a route to Jeremiah Lime's place. I am riding my bike, but only as far as Halvdale. From there, the bus will take me to Terre Haute, Indiana, where I'll catch a train to River City. After that, I'll walk or take a cab to Clarkson.

I don't tell Miller any of that because I'm already running late for the nine-thirty bus. I still have to wake Kyla and get her over to Loraine's, and time is burning.

"And this is your cover story?" Miller asks, holding up my note to my mother. "When you take your sister over to her sitter's early, she'll be on the phone to your mother within ten minutes."

"You got a better idea?" I ask him.

"Go wake up your sister," he says. "I'll come up with something." While I'm waking Kyla and making her breakfast, Miller paces the living room. "Okay, I've got it," he says. "My brother's starting his first day as counselor at Camp Chi today. Two junior counselors didn't show up, and we're helping him out overnight. It came up all of a sudden!"

"What do you mean 'we'?" I ask him.

"I'm going with you," he says. "I'll get my stuff and be back in ten minutes."

"I don't need any help," I tell him.

"Obviously, you do," he replies. "Start by tearing up that note and writing another while I'm gone."

And so, twenty minutes later, I leave Kyla at Loraine's along with a story about taking the bus to Camp Chi for an overnighter. Kyla whispers, "Good luck," as I pull out from Loraine's driveway.

Miller's waiting up the road, and he's already slowing me down. I forgot how much biking I've been doing lately. Miller hasn't and it shows. He pedals like a senior citizen. Plus, he's packed enough stuff for a week's vacation, and he's trying to balance a suitcase-sized backpack on his handlebars.

On the way to the station, Miller talks about how we're going to grab Blue and make a Hollywood getaway when we get to Indiana. *If* we get to Indiana, I say, but he doesn't get the hint.

We miss the bus.

The next one to Terre Haute is a three-hour wait, at 12:30. Okay, I'm still on schedule, just a later schedule. Taking the 12:30 bus means catching the 4:15 train from Terre Haute to River City. We'll still get to Lime's place tonight, but a few hours later than planned.

During the bus ride, I tell Miller everything I know and don't know about Mr. Lime. How his son called about their "missing dog," and how, a couple of days later, they showed up and tried to steal Blue. I tell him about Josie and the shotgun, and my fight with Daryl—that one really gets his attention.

"You know, I'm always telling you to stop fighting, but punching Daryl, that's awesome." Then he asks about the plan.

"What plan?" I answer.

"You don't have a plan?" he asks.

"Well, the plan is . . . No I don't have an exact plan, yet, but I'll come up with something." For a second, I watch Miller thinking—maybe that being a counselor at his brother's camp is a better idea than a trip to Indiana.

For most of the ride we eat snacks from the bus station vending machine and watch the other passengers and read comic books and sleep. Miller just about breaks his neck trying to catch a glimpse of the girlie magazine the guy in front of us is reading. Someone behind us is smoking a cigar and it takes me ten minutes to figure out how to open our window. When I do, the smoker complains about the breeze, and I have to shut it again. No time is spent on coming up with a plan to rescue Blue.

At Terre Haute, we jump off the bus and race across town to the train station. We arrive with five minutes to spare, enough time to buy two tickets to River City and hit the bathroom.

After splashing my face with cold water, I come out and find Miller ogling the girlie magazines at the newsstand. Telling me he's glad I'm here, he brings a *Playboy* to the cashier, points at me, and says, "My friend will pay for it."

The old guy behind the counter frowns. "Got any ID?" he asks.

Miller feels around in his pockets. "Gosh, I forgot my wallet. How old do you have to be?"

"Eighteen," the guy says.

"Oh good," Miller replies with a sigh. "I turned eighteen last week."

"Yeah, me too," the old man sneers, and grabs the magazine from his hand.

Handing Miller his bag, I pull him toward the platform. The train's about to leave, and we climb aboard for the three-and-a-half-hour ride to River City.

As we roll eastbound into Indiana, I'm thinking about Jeremiah Lime. His town, Clarkson, sits about four miles outside River City. I'm guessing Lime's a farmer because of that sticker on his pickup and because of all the open spaces surrounding Clarkson on the map.

He probably raises crops on his farm and hosts dogfights there too. So what's the connection to Chicago? Maybe, to the people who do it, dogfighting is like a sport, and they travel from town to town to compete.

Yesterday, I was planning on punching Lime and his son in the face, grabbing Blue, and making a run for it, but I know it won't be that easy. To be honest, I'm hoping that Lime is away in Chicago or some other town and Blue is alone on the farm just waiting for me to come and rescue him. A lot easier for everyone involved.

Miller gets up and walks to the end of the train car. He disappears for a few minutes before coming back smelling like a cigarette. "Were you smoking?" I ask him.

"Maybe," he says.

"Okay, first off, where?"

"In the bathroom," he replies. "Duh."

"They have a bathroom on the train?" I ask, amazed.

"Yeah," he says. "Some of these people are going to the East Coast. You think they're going to hold it all the way?"

"I was wondering why you didn't go at the station," I tell him.

"This isn't the little local train. This thing'll take you all the way to New York," he says. "Haven't you ever gone anywhere before?"

"Not really," I say. "And you shouldn't be smoking in there. You'll get us thrown off the train."

"Well, I can't smoke out here," he says. "I'm not old enough."

I shake my head and go back to my maps while Miller puts his head down and falls asleep. I'm thinking about our arrival time. We'll be pulling into River City about eight o'clock on a Friday night. Not too late, but almost dark. Not having a plan is coming back to haunt me, like, for instance, not knowing how to get Blue home once I grab him from Lime's place.

On the bus, I asked the driver if dogs were allowed, and he said no. Same thing at the train station when I bought our tickets: no dogs allowed. I think I have an idea for our return trip though, and it's all because of Ray. Since he quit drinking, he won't be at the tavern tonight. I thought I'd call and ask if he could drive to Indiana and pick us up.

A lot to ask, but I repeat the same promise I made to God—not to ask for anything else for a while. Also, I can ask Ray if he's heard from my mother. I don't think our story about working as junior counselors is going to fool anyone for too long, especially if Miller didn't leave a note that matches mine. I'll ask him when he wakes up.

The conductor calls "River City," and I shake Miller. Grabbing our bags, we step off the train into a beautiful late spring night. A full moon is rising in the east as the sun sets in the west. I must have Mr. Lime on the brain because I swear I can see a gray pickup rolling like a ghost right down Main Street, about fifty yards ahead of us. The truck turns neon red in the reflection of a bowling alley sign before disappearing around a corner.

Miller asks how far to Lime's place, and I tell him four miles. I ask if he left a note before leaving home, and he says he did. Shoving all my loose change into a nearby pay phone, I rehearse what to say. When Ray picks up, I ask if he can do me a favor.

"Let 'er rip," he says.

"My friend and I volunteered to help out at his brother's summer camp tonight, as counselors, overnight," I say.

"Congratulations," Ray says. "Anything else?"

"Well, yeah, they maybe screwed up, and they might not have a place for us to stay, and we might want to come home, so I was wondering . . ."

"If I could pick you up," he says, finishing my sentence.

"Yeah, maybe, but I won't know for an hour or two, so it would be a late night." Ray sounds suspicious, but agreeable. He says he'll be home and to call back if I need him. "So we might, but we might not . . ." I'm rushing it. The words are coming too fast, and I finally hear myself saying, "Okay, thanks, gotta go," before hanging up.

"Smooth," says Miller. I tell him to shut up.

"Now what?" he asks.

"We take a cab," I say.

"And then what? Knock on Lime's door and ask if he's got your dog?"

I've got to admit, Miller has a point. We'll have to get a ride to somewhere near his place and finish on foot. Then we can watch his property and wait for a chance to sneak in, and—

Miller interrupts my thinking. "I'm hungry," he says. Me too, but I don't want to admit it.

"And about tonight," Miller says. "Most of these old country boys keep a shotgun handy, and *that's* not going to help any." He points to the full moon climbing steadily overhead. There's not a cloud in the sky.

I think it'll be easier to free Blue at night than in broad daylight, and Miller agrees with me. "But what about tomorrow night?" he says. Or tomorrow during the day, I'm thinking.

Right now, we're both hungry and tired, and we didn't come all this way to get chased off by a shotgun-toting farmer. Better to wait until morning when we can pass by Lime's place and have a look around in daylight. Then we can decide whether to make our move in the daytime or wait until nightfall.

Heading up Main Street toward the town square, I see a "Vacancy" sign on the River City motel. It looks like we're in luck because right across from the motel is a restaurant and it's open. The sign on the restaurant flashes "EAT."

"They're everywhere," Miller says.

FORTY

I wake to someone knocking on our motel room door. All through the night, Miller snored, and when he wasn't snoring, he tossed and turned, and when he wasn't tossing and turning, he got up to smoke a cigarette in the dark. Now it's eleven o'clock, and the cleaning lady wants to know if we're leaving soon.

"Five minutes," I shout through the door, and the cleaning cart rolls away. I pull off Miller's blanket, and he sits up in bed, looking confused. I tell him we overslept. He blinks. "We're in Indiana," I say, and he mumbles, "Indiana, right."

Last night, we paid for our room, then headed over to the River City EAT for a late dinner. The man at the motel didn't want to give us a room, but Miller told him our mothers were meeting us here in the morning, and he believed it. Plus, I think we're too young to be the kind of "teenage troublemakers" that he doesn't like to rent his rooms to.

The restaurant was getting ready to close and had just three or four choices left. None of them looked very good on the menu, and they weren't. Miller laughed and said, "Whatever doesn't kill me makes me stronger."

I thought, even if that's true it probably shouldn't apply to dinner.

In our room, I notice a pop-up card in the shape of a taxi with "River City Cab" printed on it. I tell Miller it seems like our best bet to get to Seven Hills Road. "Yeah, unless the cab driver is his cousin or something," he says.

"I thought of that," I say. "There's a winery about a half mile past Lime's place where they give tours and tastings. We'll have the cab take us there."

"Right, two thirteen-year-olds going to a winery," he says.

"Speak for yourself," I tell him. "I'm fourteen. Anyway, we can say we're meeting our mothers there, too."

The cleaning lady comes back. We pack up quick and walk across the parking lot for breakfast. Even though we ate dinner late last night, I'm starving.

I order bacon and eggs with toast and potatoes, courtesy of Mr. Lime. The waitress tells me we're too late. They're already serving lunch.

Breakfast or lunch, it doesn't matter. I eat my cheeseburger so fast I can barely taste it, which is probably a good thing. Miller finishes every last bite of his triple-decker sandwich. I guess lunch, even at this place, won't kill him—maybe it'll make him stronger.

Miller asks when the coroner's inquest is and I tell him Monday, less than forty-eight hours from now. He wants to know if I'm nervous, and I don't know how to answer. I mean, yeah sure, but also I can't wait for the whole thing to be over. If it is almost over.

Right now, I just want to concentrate on what we came here for, to get Blue and get back home. All in one piece, if possible.

While we eat, we talk about our fathers. I know Miller has some kind of guilt thing about wishing his father would die and then he did. But I don't know why. Maybe there's something wrong with me because I don't feel that way about my father. Mostly, I worry about my mother and sister, and sometimes even myself. My uncle Ray, not so much anymore because he seems to be turning things around.

I don't say it out loud, but I don't miss Miller's father either. Why would I, right? But sometimes you stop by a friend's house and their father or stepfather is all friendly and asks how you've been and how your family's doing. Miller's father wasn't that type of guy.

Back outside, I think about walking to Lime's farm, but we've wasted enough time already. What if Lime's out running errands and right now is the perfect time to grab Blue? I'll never know if I don't get out there and have a look. And I'll never get there if I'm walking down some country road all day.

Instead of calling for a cab, we decide to check the train station a block away. Cabs usually seem to hang around bus depots and train stations looking for fares, so that's our first stop.

Heading up Main Street, I see a cab parked outside the station. We'll tell the driver to take us to the Seven Hills Winery. On the way past, I'll look for Lime's place. Then we'll walk back and pick a spot to see without being seen. And afterward? I guess I'll figure that out when I get there.

The cab driver, Joe, turns out to be someone's cousin all right, but not Jeremiah Lime's. He's related to the people who own the winery and blabs about it all the way there. Why he thinks two kids would be interested in his cousin's wines is a mystery to me, but most things adults do are a mystery to me. He tells us all about the great red wines and white wines and in-between wines they make.

I study Mr. Lime's farm while Miller pretends to listen to Joe. The look of the place surprises me, and I try to remember everything I see for later. When we arrive at the winery, Joe hands me a coupon for a free tour, and I hand him most of what's left of Lime's money.

After Joe's cab disappears over the hills, we turn around for a look at the winery. It looks like a nice place.

I ask Miller if he wants to go inside and buy a bottle of wine—now that he's eighteen and all. He tells me to shut up and we grab our packs and start the half-mile walk back to Lime's farm. I stuff Joe's coupon into my pocket, Miller adjusts his sliding backpack, and off we go.

I think about Lime's farm as we walk. All the other farms we pass have planted fields of corn and soybeans and gravel roads leading to farmhouses that have a "come in and say hello" kind of look. Not Lime's place.

Lime's property has a gravel road, like his neighbors', but his is blocked by a tall iron gate. Wrapped around the base of the gate is a thick chain secured with a padlock. A small forest of Oaks hides the house and barn. Glimpses of buildings appear between the trees like looking at somebody's yard through a picket fence. If his neighbors' places seem to say, "Come on in," Lime's says, "Keep out!"

I can't stop thinking about that gate. Is it there to keep visitors out, dogs in, or both?

And what's with those trees? Most farmers plant crops, not trees. It's starting to look like Jeremiah Lime isn't "most farmers." But maybe the trees are a good thing. If they help to hide Lime's property from the outside world, maybe they can hide us, too.

Closer now and I can hear dogs barking. Half a dozen, at least. Is one of them Blue? I'm not sure if I hear him or imagine it, but I swear he's in there.

I worry that Miller and I are pretty exposed out here on the road. Two kids carrying their belongings and walking down a country road miles from town—not good. If we can reach the trees without being seen, we can hide underneath and get a look at the house, maybe even climb up and get a view from above. But for the next twenty yards, all we can do is keep walking.

When I turn to have a look, what I see is definitely not good. Miller's wrestling with his backpack, which is half-open with clothes starting to spill out. Just this morning, I thought of asking him to come all the way out here on foot. I might as well have asked him to walk from Halvdale.

But we make it.

Once we're under the trees, we sit down, and I open one of our two canteens that I filled at the motel. Miller reaches in his pocket for a cigarette, but I stop him. "Hey," he complains, "we're on break, remember?"

"How I spent my summer vacation—in jail," I tell him. I remember always being able to smell my uncle smoking from our front porch whenever he stepped out for some "fresh air." I don't want that same smell to carry into Lime's house and tell him we're here.

I don't know why I'm being so hard on Miller except that I'm nervous. And I don't know what to do next, except, like he said yesterday, knock on Lime's door and ask for my dog back. Maybe I'm taking it out on him that I don't have a plan.

It's time to make one.

There's just enough room to move around underneath the trees.

As quiet as we can, Miller and I crawl from one end of the little forest to a spot on the other end where we can see the barn and sheds. Dogs are barking, but that doesn't bother me. I know from working at the shelter that sometimes dogs just bark. It doesn't mean that Jeremiah Lime or his son will come running out to see why.

Probably just the opposite. If he's the kind of man I think he is, Lime's dogs could bark all day and he wouldn't care.

I climb halfway up a big oak and look down on the whole layout. I can't see anyone, but someone shouts, "Shut up," and the dogs get quiet for a minute. The gray pickup is parked in the yard. We're at the right place, which is good. But Lime is home, which is not.

I see tractor tires and chains and hear barking, so it seems pretty clear that Lime is training dogs here.

So now we know. Some more bad news: it's getting hot, even in the shade, we're halfway through our second canteen, and I still can't figure out a way to get in and look for Blue without waiting for dark—still a long way off.

Miller stands and straightens his back and whispers up to me. He thinks we should walk back to the winery for more water and snacks before they close for the day. "Right, just step out on the road and risk being seen," I snap at him.

"It's better than sitting here thirstin' to death and waiting to get caught," he snaps back.

We're trying to argue and keep our voices down at the same time. It seems like Miller's looking for a fight, but maybe I am too. I climb down to face him, and over the next couple of minutes, a lot of stupid things get said by both of us. Things like how he's always holding me back, or how I'd have never gotten a room without him, or how I'm always complaining about him when he's trying to help, and on and on.

I'm hot and mad, and, finally, I do what I always do. I grab his shirt with my left hand and make a fist with my right. "You gonna hit me too?" he asks. We stare at each other a few seconds before I push him away.

I look down at the ground, and when I look up again, Miller's gone. I watch him stepping from the trees. He slings the canteen strap over one shoulder, his backpack over the other, and walks to the edge of the road. He's moving fast as he heads off toward the winery.

"Why couldn't he walk like that before?" I think.

Hurrying back up the tree, I look to see if anyone is following. No one is.

For the next couple of hours, I watch the house and argue with myself about whether Miller will be back. Did he really leave for fresh water, or will he call a cab when he gets to the winery and hightail it back to the train station?

If he needed water, why not stop at one of those friendly-looking farms just up the road? Probably because only the winery has a pay phone. It doesn't matter anyway. I'm alone and out of water, and if I'm waiting for anyone to come along and help me, I'll be waiting a long time.

I feel like I'm dreaming again. Every time I think of approaching the shed where the dogs are kept, Lime, his son, or a small man in city clothes steps from the house for some chore or another. Sometimes, they cross to the barn, sometimes the shed, and, once in a while, they do some actual farm work. All of it keeps me in the trees, waiting.

Then I get lucky.

Lime's son steps out of the shed and into the yard. He walks back toward the house alongside the small man. They leave the shed door open behind them, and I can see a row of cages, like at Josie's only cramped and dirty-looking.

Seven dogs in seven cages. I get the feeling there's at least that many across the aisle, hidden from view. Is Blue in one of them?

Tired of waiting, I climb down from the tree and head for the shed door.

FORTY-ONE

Unusual things are happening on the farm.

Blue is picking up vibrations everywhere and the hairs on his neck and back stand on end. Sounds and smells flood his senses. For a moment, he thinks he can smell Spence in the area, but only for a moment and then not again. But there are other signs throughout the day.

Sometime after midday, he hears two boys talking. One of the boys sounds like Spence, and Blue thinks of barking out his location. But the boys' voices turn suddenly angry and that frightens him, so he lies silently in his crate, waiting, watching, listening.

Throughout the day, the bad man makes many trips to the shed and barn. Blue can sense his nervous energy. The man starts, stops, forgets something, and retraces his steps back to where he started. His voice is sharp and his motions quick. Often, that means a night of fighting is coming.

In the heat of the afternoon, the little man crosses the yard. That man only appears on fight nights, in clothes that smell of the city. The city man is hard to read; he pays little attention to the dogs as he goes about his chores. The animals are like pieces of furniture to him. Just the fact that he's here has the dogs agitated.

But the strongest feeling comes from the boy. He speaks to the man in the usual way, in his usual voice, but there is nothing usual in his manner. His body is coiled with energy, like a dog who's been kept in his crate too long, and Blue thinks he might explode.

The man doesn't see it, Blue is sure of that, but there is a lot the man doesn't see.

Blue hopes that one day, one of the things he doesn't see will be his undoing.

The man counts too much on being the alpha of the pack. He thinks that an alpha dog leads through fear. He doesn't know a true leader does so with his eyes and his body language. He establishes an order for the pack to follow and leads with confidence, not cruelty.

Blue decides that if he's brought out to fight tonight, he'll run. Having escaped once before, he's learned a new way of thinking. Now he knows there are other types of humans in the world, and dogs that never have to fight.

He also knows that if the man catches him he'll be killed. He has to be careful and so he waits. Blue's been waiting since the day he was born, so one more day shouldn't be too difficult.

FORTY-TWO

Inside the shed, I look for Blue. I can't believe my luck because there he is in the third cage on the left. He sees me and barks and that sets off a chain reaction of barking and yelping. I have to think fast.

If I grab Blue from his cage, the only way out of here is back down Seven Hills Road—four miles to town. If Lime notices Blue's cage is empty, we'll be sitting ducks out on the road.

If I want to call a cab, the closest spot is the winery. That's if they're still open, and if I can make it that far without being seen. That's a lot of ifs. The dogs are barking louder now. I panic and turn for the safety of the trees. Just in time, because here comes Lime's son to check on the noise. All I can do is sit and wait.

The sun is low in the sky when I hear a car entering the yard. How did it get through the gate? Crawling to a spot behind the shed, I peek out as a county sheriff steps from his patrol car and knocks on Lime's front door.

Jeremiah Lime, the guy who stopped by the shelter, the guy whose address is on the slip of paper in my backpack, the guy who most definitely kidnapped Blue, answers the door. Somebody called to report him! Miller maybe, or maybe Josie's cousin. With a grin, I angle from the shed toward the house.

I'm around the corner from the porch, close enough to hear the two men talking without being seen. They sound like old pals.

"The dogs have been barking all afternoon," Lime says. "Might be a critter, might be a visitor."

"I got a call from his mother a while back," the sheriff replies. "If he's not here already, he's on his way."

I catch on pretty quickly that this isn't an arrest. The sheriff pushes his hat back on his head, and Lime smiles from the half-open screen door. "Did you really steal his dog?" the sheriff asks, chuckling.

"More like stole him back," Lime says.

Lime asks the sheriff if he's going to watch the gate tonight.

"Like always," the sheriff replies. Turning, I slow-walk back toward the tree line. If Miller can make himself invisible out on the road, maybe I can do the same here in the yard. Breathe easy, in through the nose, out through the lips. The next thing I hear is "Freeze!" I turn around to face the sheriff, all hat, sunglasses, and gun.

While the sheriff places me in handcuffs, I see something, or someone, moving underneath the trees. It's Miller. He's watching as the sheriff drags me to his patrol car and tosses me inside.

I wonder how much he heard.

Maybe he can make his way to a neighboring farmhouse and call. Who? Not the sheriff's office, that's for sure. I wouldn't blame him if he just ran back to town and caught the last train home.

I move around in the cruiser's back seat trying to get comfortable; not easy with my hands cuffed behind me. The sheriff watches in his rearview mirror.

"You alone out here?" he asks.

I look back and can just make out his eyes. I know you never lie to a cop. I know it from the Oaks. I even know it from my father's cop shows. If you lie about something, you might get away with it for a while, but pretty soon the lie catches up with you and things are worse than before.

I know what I'm supposed to say: "No, sir, my friend's in those trees back there." I figure if I don't tell the truth now, I'll be in real trouble later. Then I think, "I'm handcuffed in the back seat of a patrol car, how much more trouble could I be in?"

I stare at the sheriff's reflection in the mirror. "Yeah," I say, "except for my dog, who's in that farmer's shed back there."

The sheriff laughs. "Jeremiah's got a lot of dogs at his place, not yours though."

I know he's lying, and I wonder if he knows the same about me.

I heard him talking to Lime earlier and something isn't right. This sheriff doesn't act like either of the cops who stopped by our trailer, or even the one who stood in the judge's chambers watching over everything. The way this sheriff talks tells me that he and Lime are in the dogfighting business together. He even has a key to Lime's gate. And that makes it all right to lie. "It's only a lie if you don't believe me," Ray always says.

"Are you taking me to jail?" I ask.

"No, I'm taking you to the train station. Your mother's been calling about you," he says. "If you promise to behave yourself, I'll take off the cuffs and you can wait for her there."

"I promise," I reply.

Another lie. I'm already planning the best way back to Lime's farm.

If I call Joe the cab driver and tell him I'm low on money but can pay him later, would he drive me?

If the sheriff left me alone with his car running, could I jump in the front seat and make it back to Seven Hills Road?

There's a lot more gadgets in a police car than our station wagon: switches for the lights and siren, the two-way radio, not to mention the shotgun locked into a rack on the floor. But the steering wheel, gas pedal, and brakes all look the same.

The sun is setting as we pull into town. The sheriff calls his office on the two-way. A woman answers, and he tells her to call my mother. The woman says, "Yes, sir, Sheriff Robertson."

Earlier, I'd heard this sheriff, Robertson, tell Lime he'd already talked to my mother. What kind of lies did he tell her? Something else I heard really caught my attention. That was when Lime asked if he'd be watching the gate tonight. "Like always," Robertson said.

What kind of cop watches a gate in the middle of nowhere on a Saturday night? What other farmer even has a gate? I'm sure tonight is a big night at Lime's farm, and I don't think a big night means watching the corn grow. It can only mean dogfighting.

I picture myself crashing through Lime's gate in the sheriff's cruiser. I drive straight to the shed where Blue and the other dogs are locked in their cages. Then I grab Blue and set the other dogs free before ramming into Lime's pickup on my way back out of the yard.

I'm still daydreaming about it when we get to the train station.

The sheriff gets out, opens the back door, and takes off my handcuffs. His patrol car idles while I rub my wrists and he puts the cuffs back on his belt. "I see you anywhere but this train station tonight and you're going to jail, you got it?"

I stare at the open door of the cruiser, guessing how long it would take to jump in and drive away before he'd start shooting.

"You got it?" he repeats.

"You won't see me," I say.

The station's deserted and the ticket window is closed for the night. I drink about a gallon of water from the fountain. There's a pay phone, and, just for a second, I think about Alicia. But, right now, if I'm going to call anyone, it's got to be someone who can get me, Miller, and hopefully Blue, back home.

I'm out of change, so I call collect and listen as the operator asks Ray if he'll accept the charges for a long-distance call.

"You bet," he answers, and, half begging, half explaining, I ask my uncle if he can drive to River City, Indiana, and pick me up at the train station. "On my way," he says.

It's four miles back to Lime's place and getting dark. There are four ways to get there that I know of: drive, bike, run, or walk. Driving is faster than biking, which is faster than running, which is faster than walking. I can walk there in a little over an hour or run that far in a little over a half hour. So that's the plan. I'll leave the station and run to Lime's farm. If I come across an unlocked bike, or, better still, a car with the keys in it, I'll be there in no time.

I'm not worried about the sheriff, figuring he's already halfway back to Lime's farm to guard his stupid gate. Just in case, I peek out the station window before opening the door.

FORTY-THREE

Main Street looks the same as the night before.

A block to the east are the River City version of EAT and the motel. A little out of my way, but I remember something. Last night, crossing from the motel, I noticed a bike leaning against the kitchen door of the restaurant. During our meal, there was a kid our age cleaning tables and washing dishes. The bike must be his.

If he's working again tonight, I'll borrow his bike and start my trip to Lime's farm.

Okay, technically I'm stealing the bike. But I'll bring it back later, and what's the harm anyway? If Robertson sees me anywhere in town, bike or no bike, he's taking me to jail, so "borrowing" a bike will be the least of my problems.

When I get to the restaurant, the bike's still there, looking like it hasn't been moved since the night before. Maybe it hasn't. But there's air in the tires and the chain looks good, so I roll it quietly away from the building and back up Main Street.

The sky is silver-dark under a full moon. Heading south toward Lime's farm, I follow the white stripes painted down the center of Seven Hills Road. Craning my head around, I look for headlights from either direction. Any sign of a car and I'll pull off into the ditch.

Miller sees me before I see him. "In here," he whispers, and I roll the bike off the road and into the trees. There's no reason to hide it, and with any luck, we'll be out of here soon.

Trying to catch my breath and keep my voice down at the same time, I ask if he's seen anything.

"Plenty," he says. "Where did he take you? I thought you'd be in jail by now."

"Just the station," I say, and thank him for coming back.

"Yeah, I waited for a train," he says, "but when it came, I didn't get on." He tells me I owe him "big time." I remind him what a great essay he's going to have for

"How I Spent My Summer Vacation." Then he fills me in on what's been happening at Mr. Lime's this Saturday night.

"First, a couple of cars arrived. Two cars, with two guys and two dogs inside each one. They just sat there at the gate, talking and drinking beer for a while, until they started beeping their horns and yelling for someone to let them into the yard."

"Then what?" I ask him.

"Then the sheriff got back, without you. See his cruiser parked over there?"

By crawling a couple of feet, I can see Robertson's car parked to the side of Lime's driveway. There's no sign of the sheriff though, and that worries me. Miller keeps going with his story. "The sheriff got out of his car and chewed the guys out good for making so much noise. He asked them if they wanted to turn around and go back where they came from or behave themselves in his county.

"That quieted them down. Then he opened the gate and let those two carfuls inside. But he closed it again, right behind them."

"Damn" is all I can say.

Miller says that during all of this, Lime's dogs were barking from the shed at the dogs in the cars, who barked back. There were a lot of "shut ups," before the guys reached in their back seats and slapped the dogs to quiet them down.

"I think they're all drunk," he tells me. While I'm trying to decide if the men being drunk is good or bad for us, a pickup arrives with two guys up front and two dogs in cages in the back.

Robertson steps out of the shadows and approaches the pickup. He talks to the men inside. I can't make out what they're saying, but pretty soon the gate swings open and the truck rolls slowly into the yard.

Another car pulls into the driveway. Whatever's happening here tonight is happening soon. Now there's even more activity: Lime's son leaves the house and crosses the yard toward the barn. I tell Miller that when Lime, his son and the small man are all in the barn, the house will be empty.

"So?" he says.

"So," I tell him, "at some point tonight, we need the sheriff there to go away. And we're going to need more than a bicycle to get back to town."

"What do you want me to do?" he asks.

"You're smart," I say, "think of something." I crouch down and start my journey toward the other end of the trees.

"Where are you going?" Miller whispers after me.

"I'm going to get my dog."

Kneeling under the last tree, I'm close to the shed and far from the sheriff.

The men from the pickup uncrate their dogs and let them run around the yard. In the distance, I can see the headlights of another vehicle, a station wagon, with two men in the front seat. I wait until the wagon turns its lights off before sticking my head out of the trees.

The station wagon has two dogs in its back seat and when the guys let them out, one snarls at the dogs from the pickup. All the dogs are nervous and excited and snapping at one another. The men laugh until the snarling gets worse. Out of nowhere, the driver of the pickup begins whipping his dog with a leather leash he's holding.

After that it gets quiet—until someone laughs, and then they're all laughing again. I take a breath before dashing across the open space to the back of the barn.

Even from here, I can hear the dogs in the shed. They're barking like crazy, all worked up and howling at any nearby movement. Right now, there's a lot of movement. Behind the barn, I look for an opening.

The back door is unlocked, and I take a look inside. More people with more dogs are arriving every minute. In addition to the guys from the pickup, the first carload of men is already milling around inside. Half of them look drunk, and one is prodding a dog with a stick. The place is filling up quick.

There's one woman, seven or eight men, and a dozen dogs now. The dog being prodded finally turns and lunges at the man with the stick. The other men hoot and howl. A lot of time is spent sizing up one another's animals. Sometimes, two dogs get too close to each other and that sets off another round of snarling.

Lime's son enters and gestures to a cooler nearby, and all the men, but not the woman, help themselves to a cold beer.

There are a lot of dogs in the barn, but no Blue. I have to get back to the shed. Peeking out from behind the barn, I wait for a chance to cross. That's when I see Lime.

He's walking from the house and stopping to talk with a couple of late arrivals who are parking their cars and trucks. I hear the same loud voice I remember from the shelter, and I can see why he hosts these dogfights. He likes being a big shot.

I bet he gets a kick out of making people wait at his gate.

Behind him, I see Miller slipping into the empty farmhouse. I wonder about the sheriff and where he goes after everyone is inside. He's in uniform, so I guess he's on duty. Hopefully, that means he'll just drive away and do some sheriff thing after everyone's settled into the barn.

I'm wasting too much time thinking, and when it looks like the coast is clear, I turn for the shed.

I freeze as the little man in city clothes steps out of the shed with two dogs on leashes: a big Boxer and Blue. They're heading back to the barn and I can only guess what that means.

With my back against the barn wall, I slump to the ground and feel like crying. I waited too long.

FORTY-FOUR

Wandering around the yard, I find myself standing outside the shed. Stepping in, I wait while my eyes adjust to the darkness. I bump up against something, a cage, and the dog inside licks my fingers.

I think about my chances. There's one of me—two if you count Miller, but he was never any good in a fight—against a dozen drunken, angry men.

All around me is the smell of dirt and fear. The only light is the moon slanting through the shed door. Swinging the door all the way open, I can make out the shadows of dogs turning restlessly in their cages.

I find the switch for an overhead light. The brightness surprises me and I can see the faces of nine or ten dogs, all looking back at me. They're wagging their tails and whimpering, probably hoping that this is the day that someone opens their cage and plays with them.

How long have some of them been wondering that?

I might still have a little time. Even if Blue and the Boxer are Mr. Lime's first two dogs of the night, it doesn't mean that either of them is in the very first fight. I wonder how long a dogfight lasts? Anywhere from a minute to an hour, I guess.

Then I think, now or half an hour from now, what's the difference? I remember Lime pretending to be reasonable the day he tried to steal Blue. Would he pretend again if I challenged him in front of all these witnesses? He'd probably call Robertson to handle any trouble. But is Robertson still here?

I try to think, but my head is spinning. I don't have a plan because what plan could there ever be except to swoop in, grab Blue, and run like hell.

I'm tired of thinking. And hiding. And lying. And getting arrested by a man who should be arrested himself. I lift my fingers to the dog that licked them earlier and open his cage. Moving down the line, I open all the cages. One at a time the dogs step out, some carefully, some like they've been sprung from prison.

Finding a bag of dog food, I pour it into a big pile on the ground. Then I fill a couple of bowls with water from a hose. The dogs eat and drink and run in circles like they haven't done any of those things in a long time.

Heading for the barn, I remember my first day at Josie's shelter. How the dogs jumped and bounced off my legs like pinballs, all wanting to play. Halfway across the yard, I'm shaken from my memory by the red flashing of police lights and I know playtime's over. I turn around to face the sheriff.

Instead, I see Miller. He's running from the house, grinning from ear to ear. Turning again, I'm amazed at the sight of Robertson's car pulling away from the gate and taking off down Seven Hills Road. My heart is pounding like race day in gym class. "Did you do that?" I ask Miller.

"I called in about a guy with a knife, a gun, and a bomb at this restaurant on the other side of the county," he says, all proud.

"A bomb?" I say. Miller just shrugs. "What about a car?"

"No, I didn't mention a car," he tells me, and we both crack up laughing right there in the yard. "I found these in the house," he says, holding up a key ring. "No car keys, though."

"Any car—as long as it's an automatic," I say. "Unless you can drive stick shift."

"I can barely drive an automatic," he tells me, and he heads off in the direction of the parked cars. The dogs, most of them, stay with me.

At the barn door, I stand to one side, trying to hide and look for Blue at the same time. That's impossible though with Lime's dogs jumping and barking all around me, so I take a step inside. In the pit, the Boxer is battling with a big Doberman that I'd seen arriving earlier. Everyone is cursing and yelling and placing bets like they're watching a football game on TV. The woman yells the loudest, like maybe she has to make up for being the only female around.

The dogs sitting near their masters go crazy at the sight of Lime's dogs, even the dogs in the pit stop and turn in my direction. The barn goes dead quiet. Everyone stares at Lime's dogs—and me.

And then they start to laugh.

Blue sees me and pulls at his leash. He's clawing at the ground, and Lime's son has a hard time holding him back. Lime doesn't like what he's seeing, and he doesn't like the laughter. He lunges for Blue's leash, but he's concentrating on me, and Blue breaks free. He runs over to meet me and I rub his ears and neck while he licks my face.

Lime is on us in a heartbeat. I push Blue behind me, thinking that Lime wants to snatch him back. But it isn't Blue he's after. He wants me. Lime pulls back a big fist and is about to swing when he notices everyone in the barn staring at him. He wants to hit me all right, but he isn't dumb enough to do it in front of all these witnesses.

Stepping back, he grabs his son by the arm and shoves him in my direction, shouting, "Caleb, he's stealing our dog!"

That's smart. It makes everyone in the crowd think I'm the thief, not them. Lime's son stares at his father. I can almost hear him thinking, "Wait, didn't we just steal this dog from him?" It doesn't matter though because Lime pushes him harder and says, "Get my dog back, and get him out of here!"

Lime's son hustles over and tries to reach around me for Blue. But Blue's quick, and I'm turning in half circles, using my body to block his path. He's turning too, and getting frustrated, until finally his father shouts, "Hit him."

"Hit him," someone in the crowd echoes, and a few others pick up the chant. "Hit him, hit him!" I guess if they can't have their dogfight, they'll settle for two people in the center of the pit.

"Let him have it," the woman shouts, and Lime's son advances on me. He aims a right hand at the left side of my face, but I lean away and the punch catches mostly air. Then he tries a left hand with the same result. Somebody snickers, and I can see his eyes flash with anger. He swings again, harder this time, but the punch just grazes my shoulder.

I think of the lessons I learned from my father: how to hit, how to take a hit, and how to feel trouble coming by that weird electricity in the air when something bad is about to happen. Something bad is happening now.

Blue's running back and forth behind me, and from the corner of my eye I see Lime moving in to grab him. The Boxer who's been watching all this clamps down on Lime's pant leg and won't let go. Jumping up, the Doberman grabs his shirt cuff and hangs on for dear life.

Lime twists like a crazy man and the thing he hates most is happening: people are laughing. He gives another violent shake and throws off both dogs before advancing on his son and me in the middle of the pit.

"He's taking away everything you worked for. Hit him, damn it," Lime shouts at his boy.

His son raises his fists, but his heart isn't in it. It was never his fight to begin with. His father pushes him in my direction, but with a strange calm he just lowers his hands to his sides. Bumping into Lime on his way out of the pit, he says, "You hit him." And he keeps on walking.

Lime's surprised, but too angry to stop and think. He moves in, blood boiling, fists raised. My hands curl into fists, and I circle back, ready to throw a punch. If there was ever a time I needed to fight, this is the time.

I look around the barn: at dogs scarred and bleeding, at a dozen men and one woman howling for my blood. I think back to my father, and Miller's father, and all the older guys from the Oaks, and Daryl and Teski and every other kid I ever fought, and I think: Enough.

I put my hands up close to my head and tuck my elbows in close to my ribs and let Lime swing.

He's giving me everything he's got, but most of his punches are bouncing off my hands and shoulders and elbows. The punches hurt down to my bones. But they must hurt his fists too, and he can't land a knock-out punch, against me, a kid. He's angry and losing energy. He lowers his hands for a second to catch his breath, and I do the same.

Recharged, he starts in again. I feel like my ribs are breaking. The bones in my hands and arms ache, and I don't know how much longer I can hold out. But I won't hit back. A cut on my forehead trickles blood into my eyes making it hard to see, and my nose and upper lip run red. I won't hit back. Finally, after what feels like forever, one of Lime's dogfighting buddies has seen enough. He steps between us, hands raised, and says, "Let it go, Jeremiah."

"It's just one dog," a gruff-looking old-timer chimes in.

The first guy wraps an arm around Lime and leads him over to the cooler, while the second hands him a beer. Everyone's looking at him, and me, to see what'll happen next.

I reach down with a sore arm and take Blue by his leash and rub his head. After a last look back at Lime and his low-life buddies, I whisper, "Let's go home, boy."

Stepping into the yard with Blue, I move my arms and shoulders to help with the pain and wait. I know we're being watched, so I stand still, squinting into the darkness. Just beyond the open gate, I can see a car idling in the driveway.

A few seconds later, I hear the dogfight starting up again. Someone in the barn laughs, a dog snarls, and things are returning to normal.

At the gate, I watch as the gray pickup pulls slowly from the yard. Lime's son is at the wheel. Reaching the road, he turns on his headlights and accelerates away from his father's farm. Swinging the gate closed, I slide the padlock through the chain and click it shut. When I open the car door, Blue hops in the front seat ahead of me.

"Where to?" Miller asks.

"The train station," I tell him, and he tosses Lime's key ring into the bushes. Before we can pull away, three of Lime's dogs work their way through the trees and run to the car. I open the back door and they hop inside.

Miller handles the car like he's been doing it all his life. "My brother lets me drive sometimes," he says, and we pull onto Seven Hills Road.

"Wait," I tell him, and I grab the bike from the trees and toss it in the trunk. Miller turns left for the ride to River City.

The train station's deserted and Miller says, "I don't think I can make it all the way home." We park in the lot and wait. It's a small-town Saturday night, not much traffic, and I jump every time a car turns the corner, thinking this one for sure will be the sheriff coming back to arrest us.

When we're about to give up, I see Ray's car pulling to a stop at the far end of the parking lot. Miller flashes our headlights, Ray pulls alongside, and we switch the dogs from one car to the other. I lean the bike against the restaurant wall and tell Ray to lead-foot it out of the county. "Slow is better," he says.

On the road, Ray tells us, "I'd hate to be you two right about now. I talked to both of your mothers before I left." Then he asks if either of us has a cigarette.

Josie's surprised, to say the least, when I stop by with three new dogs late on a Saturday night. She welcomes Blue back to town and asks me if I can work a full day tomorrow, washing, walking, and intaking the new arrivals. I tell her yes and promise to work lots of hours this summer to help with the extra work.

If I'm not in jail, I think, but I don't mention that part.

FORTY-FIVE

Same bailiff. Same cop. Same social worker. Same court reporter. Same judge. But this time we're all in a courtroom and not the judge's office. Also, the judge is sitting up on his bench in a black robe and he looks a lot more intimidating.

If he's got a can of Mello Yello stashed up there, I can't see it from where I'm sitting.

Because it's a coroner's inquest, there's a coroner, a doctor whose patients are all dead, like my father. That creeps me out a little. But he's not the only one the judge will be talking to. There's all those people I mentioned before, and, to be honest, the most important person here today is, well, me.

I was the last one to see my father alive, and I know the judge is going to ask a lot of questions. I've got some things to say that might surprise him, and myself too, I guess. Back at the beginning, I didn't trust myself to tell what happened. Now I think I can. I don't want a lawyer, and I don't want to hear Ray's advice, and my mother can't change my mind—I just want to tell the truth.

Even in this building, I don't think that's something they hear too often.

But if the judge wants to know what happened on "the night in question," first he's going to have to hear about a lot of other nights leading up to it. Afterward, if he sends me to juvenile hall, or jail, at least my mother and sister will be safe. They can watch Blue for me until I come back home.

Earlier, the bailiff called the session of court to order. "Hear ye, hear ye, anyone having business before this court, be recognized." Then, due to a minor being involved—me—they sealed the courtroom. Which basically means kicking out anyone who isn't involved in the case, like "trial watchers," who are people that hang around courthouses and listen to trials.

Kind of like my father with his cop shows, but in real life, not on TV.

After that, a second bailiff stood by the door to keep out anyone who might stroll in. The first bailiff said, "All rise, please," and the judge tapped his gavel on a little wooden disc on his desk to get things started. Everyone stood, except for the court reporter.

She sits through everything, probably because it's impossible to write down what everyone is saying if you're popping up and down like a jack-in-the-box. Still, she must want to get up and stretch her back every once in a while.

So now we're all sealed and seated and the judge is telling us why we're here and what to expect. "To reach a verdict on the cause of death of John T. MacElliott on the evening of May 18, 1979. Generally, we would impanel a jury, but due to the age of at least one possible witness, I am the sole arbiter in today's proceedings. Bailiff, call the first witness."

The coroner goes first. I thought he'd look like an undertaker in a horror movie, but he's a pink pudgy guy who looks like a golfer. The judge asks him a lot of easy questions, but the "bread and butter one," as Ray would say, is, "Were you able to determine a cause of death in this case?"

The coroner answers, "Yes, Your Honor, the cause of death was blunt force trauma to the head, resulting in traumatic brain injury."

The judge asks, "And the cause of this blunt force trauma?"

"Unknown, Your Honor."

After thanking him, the judge says, "Witness dismissed."

Mr. Moore is next, followed by the social worker who was out to our house about half a dozen times back in my father's worst days. Even Mr. Schmink makes a surprise appearance. None of them want to come out and say my father was a no-good drunk who deserved what happened to him. But nobody says the opposite either.

At one point, I see the judge reaching down for the Mello Yello. He takes a sip before stashing the can back out of view. Then, about twenty minutes later, after Mr. Schmink finishes up, the judge calls a recess. He says we'll meet back after lunch and hear from the remaining witnesses.

As far as I can tell that would be me and the young cop who answered the call that night.

Lunch is a quick burger and fries from Tastee-Freez and then it's back to the courtroom. The young cop is the first witness after lunch, and the judge pretty much goes over what everyone already knows. Or what they think they know.

The cop, whose name is Galfka, tells how he was the first one on the scene, how he found me beat up in the yard, how he'd been to our house for this kind of thing before, and how he went inside alone while we waited outside. Galfka's "bread and butter" question comes next.

"Was Mr. MacElliott deceased when you found him?"

"No, Your Honor."

"And yet you put in no immediate call for assistance. Why is that?"

"I found him where he fell, with his head split open from the corner of the glass coffee table."

"That's your opinion?"

"That's my opinion, yes."

"And what happened next?" the judge asks.

"He came to, a little bit, when he heard me."

"And then?"

"I rolled him over, and he asked me if he was going to die. I told him yes."

"Do you have any medical training, Officer?"

"No, Your Honor, but I've seen plenty like him before. Too many."

"Where was that?"

"Vietnam, Your Honor."

"Anything you'd like to add, Officer?"

"No, sir."

"Witness dismissed."

It's my turn. After the bailiff swears me in, the judge looks at me, half-bored and half-angry, and says, "I assume you are again incurring your right against self-incrimination?"

"No, sir."

"No, meaning you won't answer my questions, or no, you're giving up you're right not to speak?"

"I'll tell you anything you want to know," I say.

"Well, that's quite a difference from our last meeting. Has something changed?"

"Yes, sir, a lot of things," I reply.

I tell the judge that, after my father died, I figured out a way not to lie—by saying nothing. Then I add, "Saying nothing is good, but now I know a better way—just tell the truth." The judge agrees and asks me to lead him through "the events of that evening."

I start at the beginning. How I watched my father drink, even more than usual, and crush his empty beer cans in the can-crusher in the kitchen, then sit on the couch switching channels with his remote control while my mother was working at the diner and Kyla hung out at Loraine's house, a block away.

I tell the judge of my plan to get my father upset—so upset that we'd have another fight, just like the one a few weeks earlier, and the one before that, and all the others through the years.

"Why would you do that?" he asks me.

"I wanted him to come after me and knock me around a little so that I'd look beat up when I ran outside. But first I was going to crush his skull with the table leg, the one that came loose during our last fight."

I look at my mother, who's crying into her hands. Nobody else is moving, or saying a word. They're all staring back at me—and the judge.

Finally, almost in a whisper, he says, "Go on."

I tell him how I'd beaten my father in our previous fight, and I was feeling confident because of that. But I didn't want to beat him in a fight. I wanted him out of our lives forever.

I needed witnesses, and I thought I knew where to find them. Mr. Moore's Fairlane was parked in his carport, so that was one. I knew the young cop, Galfka, was on patrol. I'd seen him earlier, and I knew he'd be back on the half hour, right around the time my mother would be getting home. Daryl usually "happened to walk by" around then too, but not too close, because he was sweet on my mother and afraid of my father at the same time. And Loraine usually walked Kyla home right after nine.

With any luck, there might be a few more people passing by, but those six would have to do for a start.

The rest was easy. I watched the clock and waited, and let my father drink himself into a stupor. The only tricky part was the timing. He always had a short fuse, but how short? Was three minutes long enough? Would five be too long?

Around eight forty-five, I watched as he got up from his chair, flattened another can in the crusher, laid his remote control on the coffee table, and headed down the hall to the bathroom.

I tell the judge how I engineered the whole thing. How, when I heard him in the bathroom, I grabbed his remote and laid it in my lap and waited. Waited, while the electricity in the air ran through me and around me. Waited, and tried to control my breathing the way Mr. Schmink taught me—in through the nose, out through the lips. I didn't have to wait long.

Describing our fight, I stick to the facts and admit everything: the kicked box of cans, asking about a dog that I knew he'd never let me have, crushing his remote, all of it.

Then all my plans went out the window. He was faster and stronger than I'd remembered, probably because this time he wanted to kill me. I wasn't going to be able to get him near the coffee table and beat his brains in; I'd be lucky to get out of the trailer in one piece. That's when I knew I was fighting for my life.

I grabbed the table leg but couldn't use it at first because he had my arms pinned to my sides. We wrestled, until he slipped on a crushed can and fell to his knees on the kitchen floor. I was above him with the table leg in my right hand.

My father wrapped his arms around my legs and gasped for breath. The top of his head looked like a perfect target, the way I'd pictured it when I'd planned this thing. One good swing, maybe two, then I'd slide his body under the coffee table before running out the door. My plan could still work.

He squeezed my legs and I knew he was hanging on, catching his breath and gathering his strength before climbing to his feet and starting again. I raised the table leg high in the air and froze. I couldn't do it. One swing and my life, and my mother's and Kyla's, would be better forever. My arm wouldn't move.

I managed to peel my father off my legs. As I stumbled out of his grip, he got to his feet. Turning for the door, I could feel him right behind me. Clawing at the air, he got lucky and grabbed a fistful of my shirt collar. He began to pull me backward. I had one thought: make it to the yard. This time he was so mad, he'd surely chase me out there and continue the fight— in front of witnesses.

Using all the strength I had, I planted my feet and drove myself forward, lunging for the door. My shirt tore in his hands and he fell backward. I heard the crash behind me, but wasn't about to turn around.

I ran through the door to the porch beyond. In the yard, I breathed the fresh air while the neighbors watched, and my mother came to me, and the cop pulled to a stop in his squad car. My father never came out of the trailer. I didn't know why, and I couldn't go back inside to look, so I didn't know what had happened until the police told us later.

When I finish, it's dead quiet in the courtroom. I don't know if I've just put myself in jail by talking too much, or done the right thing by telling the truth. The judge looks at me a long time before speaking. "I have a few follow-up questions," he says.

"Your initial plan, such as it was, was to start a fight that ended with you killing your father?"

"Yes, sir. Until I punked out."

"When your first plan failed, you hoped he would chase you into the yard where witnesses would see him beating you? Afterward, you thought, maybe he would be removed from the family and the beatings of you, your sister, and mother would end?"

"I was just hoping someone would do something," I say.

"Did you strike your father first?"

"No, sir."

"Did you place something on the floor to intentionally trip him, hoping he would hit his head?"

"No, sir."

"Did you hit him in the head with any object?"

"No, Your Honor."

"At the end, did you plan for him to die?"

"I thought he might kill me, not the other way around."

"Witness dismissed."

FORTY-SIX

We called the Indiana State Police when we got home that night. They took down all our information and said they'd pay a visit to Mr. Lime and get back to us. They never did. I guess I know what that means. I wonder about Jeremiah Lime's other dogs sometimes, the ones that didn't jump in the car with Miller and me. I hope they got away.

Maybe they made it to the back doors of some nearby farmers who let them in for the night, which turned into a couple of nights and then a week and then forever.

Maybe right now some dog is running around that farmer's yard during the day and sleeping on the bed at night with the farmer and his wife even though they said at first, "No dogs on the bed." But they make an exception for this dog because "he's part of the family now."

I think about it sometimes, how the kind of man who would welcome a stray dog and love it and give it a home could live just down the road from the kind of man who would beat his wife or kids or dog. Neighbors.

I've been working at the shelter a lot lately. Summer school's started, and that's no fun, but I'm out by noon, and after lunch I pedal over to Josie's and put in a few hours before heading home to play with Blue. Sometimes, I meet Alicia at the Halvdale pool for a swim.

I like to hold my breath and go under the surface and just stay there, thinking about nothing until Alicia finally pulls me out because she thinks I'm drowning.

Coming home one day, I found Ray painting the outside of our trailer. He's building us a new porch, too.

I never noticed before, but there are a lot of nice places in the Oaks, like Mr. Moore's and Loraine's and even Miller's trailer. One of our closest neighbors has a giant vegetable garden alongside her back porch. I must have pedaled past there a hundred times before I saw it.

I never found out what was in the lawyer's letter. I think about the inquest once in a while. Did I tell the whole truth? I told the judge everything about "the night in question." I didn't tell him much about afterward or before, but he didn't ask about afterward or before.

I didn't tell him everything about the young cop, Galfka. How he amazed me by challenging my father to a fight in his own house. I'd never seen anything like that before. Until that night, I thought my father was untouchable. The alpha dog.

After that, I started to think differently about things.

I waved to Galfka whenever I saw him on patrol, and he waved back. A couple of times, he pulled over and asked how I was doing. It gave me hope.

I wasn't planning on Galfka beating up my father if he found him in the yard beating on me, but I needed someone there who would stand up to him, just in case. Just in case things didn't work out the way I'd planned. And things sure didn't work out the way I'd planned.

Galfka helped me in other ways, by giving me lots of great advice. He'd pull over and we'd talk in the days after my father died. He told me things about the law and what to watch out for in court, but mostly he just made me feel like it wasn't my fault that my father was a "no-good son of a bitch." Galfka's words, not mine.

He told me how he had a father who was the same way. He said that was why he joined the army at seventeen. "Just to get away from him."

"How was it?" I asked him once.

"Not too good," he laughed. "They sent me to Vietnam. Still, better than living with my father," he said. "I signed up for a second tour rather than going home."

That gave me hope, too, in a weird way. Knowing that he turned out all right after everything he went through with his father and fighting in the war. It made me think I could make it, too. I think Galfka was a real soldier, not the Daryl kind. One way to tell is that the guys who talk about it the most did the least, and vice versa.

When I got to know him better, I finally asked the "bread and butter question." I started by saying, "You don't have to tell me if you don't want to . . ."

He repeated what I'd told the judge. "I'll tell you anything you want to know."

So I asked, "What happened when you went inside our trailer that night?"

Galfka looked me in the eye and said, "You didn't do a damn thing wrong."

"But what does that mean?" I pressed him.

"It means," he said, "that you didn't kill him. And you're not a punk. Don't worry about him anymore. Worry about your mother, and your sister, and yourself. And your dog," he added before pulling away.

The End

Acknowledgments

Thanks to Allison Kennedy for research assistance and snappy replies. To Avner Landes, Lana Barnes, and Sarah Lahay for editorial and design brilliance. And to the thousands of volunteers at hundreds of animal rescue organizations. Thank you, all.

About the Author

Dave Schulze lives with his wife, and a rotating cast of dogs, in the suburbs of Chicago. He is the father of two grown children. *Hitter and Blue* is his first novel.

Made in the USA
Monee, IL
05 October 2024